Beyond The Pavement

by

Albert Drake

Flat Out Press

Acknowledgements:

Sections of this novel have appeared in the following magazines and anthologies: *Ante, Graffiti, Latitude* (Scott, Foresman Co.), *Quixote, Rockbottom,* and *South Dakota Review.*

ISBN: 0-936892-25-0
Library of Congress
Cataloging in Publication No.: 80-53525

Originally Published by:
The White Ewe Press

Second Edition by:
Flat Out Press
PO Box 66874
Portland, OR 97290-6874

www.flatoutpress.com

Chapter 1

The sound began as a whisper, the buzz of an annoying insect, a noise almost subliminal, and then it quickly grew to become undeniable, insistent, an element as substantial as the row of poplar trees that formed a backdrop along the old two-lane road. The sound was that of a jet plane, or of a storm approaching, although the blue sky this summer morning was clear and the weather predictable.

As the sound built in volume cows moved away from the fence, their eyes rolling in panic at the unseen danger, and then one saw the source: not a swarm of bees, nor a runaway semi-truck, but a fenderless, lowered car, angled forward as if it were literally cutting away at the wind's resistance, the lines of speed flowing from it as if this were an artist's airbrush version of what such a car should look like. In spite of the sense of speed, the car seemed, even to a person unfamiliar with cars, an anachronism, a vision from the past.

Sound built, collecting behind the machine like a great cloud of dust, and then suddenly the car was past, the noise of the open exhausts diminishing down the empty country road. But in the second of its passing one saw the flash of the chrome-plated front end and engine, and the sun glinting from the narrow, chopped windshield; one saw the driver, a kid, cap worn backward like an old-time race car driver, hunched over the steering wheel, a crazy grin on his face as if he did this all the time for pleasure, but a look of amazement, too, as if the car had been shot from a giant pistol and the driver was hanging on and steering, the car essentially out of control. Then the machine was past, the stubby rear deck bobbing, up and down as if nodding in agreement to what the front part of the car had decided to do.

Mill looked over the cowl at the left front tire and tried to hold the wheel so that that tire was right on the faded center line but the buggy spring suspension bounced wildly at every hole, throwing him sideways, the entire car rising clear of the road and falling like a ship on a rough sea. He did not remember the ride as having been so rough in the old days, nor the steering so heavy. Although he had not driven this roadster for almost seven years now, the car did not seem strange: the leather of the seat was contoured to his body, the midget race car wheel fitted under his knuckles, the familiar gauges spun like erratic compasses. Lines of speed flowed from the stamp-sized radiator and the naked front tires; wind clawed at his head and blurred his vision; the staccato exhaust was deafening.

But he loved it—the speed, the noise, the smell of gasoline and exhaust, the textures of leather, lacquer, and aluminum—and he felt pleasure rising within his chest like a powerful engine. He was back in his roadster again, and this route was his speed run, as it had been in the old days.

Seen at high speed over the abrupt cowl, the road resembled a rifled gun barrel. He approached the first curve and the high roar collected behind; a shift to second and he felt gears and tires howl in protest, the engine backfire—midway through the curve the car pivoted, turned parallel to the sun until Mill applied power to straighten the rear wheels. In the mirror he saw the long, awful slash of black, a check mark on the asphalt, and as if he were able to see beyond the mirror into the implied crash he felt fear; his hands shook but the nervous tic he had recently acquired did not tear at his cheek. Then another curve which, taken at eighty miles per hour, became a switchback; Mill felt excitement and pleasure and fear rise in his chest as he gripped the wheel, stepped on the gas, heard three carburetor mouths suck huge draughts of air. But the engine was sluggish in its wide sweep after sitting idle for seven years, and the exhaust became a flat discord. Centrifugal force drove the car toward the outside of the curve, throwing Mill to the right, the tires on that side teetering along the pavement's rim.

Then he was out of the curve and on the straight, his hand jerking the long shift lever into high gear while his foot held the gas pedal to the floor. This was his reason for coming home—to drive his old roadster flat out through the clean, clear air of dawn, down this familiar road—and he felt good.

And then, having followed the old speed run, there was nothing to do but to turn around and go back.

He let up on the pedal, the booming exhaust diminishing and then passing him; he made a U-turn and headed toward town, noticing that the gas gauge was falling toward empty. He drove slowly, and when he reached the black chevron marks his tires had left on the road all speed had passed him. Fronty's garage appeared just as the carburetors choked, yawned, and the tach fluttered wildly. *Kohlah kohl kohl awwk,* coasting down the asphalt and cramping the wheel he rolled off the apron and over loose gravel, *kohl kohl,* the engine catching, firing, then dying as it lost momentum and came to a stop one foot from the tall gravity feed gas pumps.

From the fields around the station came the clack of a million insects, but from the station itself there was only silence. Business, Mill imagined, was probably not good. He knew that Fronty was here, however, for Fronty's pickup was parked beside the office and steam filtered from its radiator; long ago, after Fronty's accident, the mechanic had fitted the truck with special hand controls, and he would never sell it. The rust-flecked oval sign at the roadside read Hudson-Terraplane and Ford specialist; Ford had survived anyway, and Mill imagined that Fronty was making enough money to pay the rent. No mention of Miller one-sticks or Hal DOCs or Offys or Cragar two ports. Almost no one remembered when Fronty had been one of the best drivers in the Northwest, before his accident, and, later, the best racing mechanic. Now he was simply a working mechanic in an edge-of-the-city two bit garage.

Mill stepped past the high, gravity feed pumps and into the office. Through the geometry of the doorway he saw the two championship cars; although they had not been off their trailers for years, they were in good shape; brilliant red and yellow paint flared at the margins of the tarps, and chrome upswept headers, muzzled with rags, gave motion to the static machinery.

Except for the confusion of tools, old parts, dark oil on the floor nothing here had changed from the time Mill had spent Saturdays listening to the bench racers—not the building, nor the two trailered race cars, nor the man who now attempted to wipe grease from the floor without falling from his wheelchair. Fronty, a fading man in faded overalls, with sandy hair and watery blue eyes below negligible eyebrows.

When the old man looked up to see the grinning boy with his crash helmet of primer black hair, he undoubtedly saw instead an earlier version, a high school kid, thin as a bumper.

"Why," he said, straightening up in the chair and wiping his hands, "why, I'll be damned. Mill." He extended his hand and when Mill grasped it he felt the bearing hardness of fingers. "Why, I'll be damned. I often wondered about you... you..."

His words came from tight, faded lips and his tone was cool, like pit signals during a serious race. For Mill had never written to the old man, and had not seen him for over seven years, before school and the army.

"How's it going, Fronty?"

The mechanic swiveled the chair and scanned the darkness: the chain hoist, heavy with its own weight; the wooden floor and walkdown lube pit, stained with dark, sweet grease. "I'm utilizing my time." His eyes slid out the window to the street and the towering green mountain beyond. Then he swung the chair back, wheeled into the office, and plugged in the hot plate.

4

Mill felt a rush of excitement, remembering the hours he had spent in this garage during the years he had been in high school, and he felt a sudden desire to relive those years in conversation but Fronty was quiet, reserved, and so Mill said nothing.

Finally, Fronty said: "So you got an education." Fronty had seen Mill come and go, and in that time had tutored him about engines. He had, in a way, contributed to the boy's education, and if there was a certain pride in his voice there was regret too—he was thinking perhaps of his own boy, who might have been a college graduate. Or at least a father, which was as good to an old man who desired grandchildren.

Neither knew how to begin. The coffee started to perk while Mill studied the photographs on the wall: photographs of men and cars, most of both gone now. There were on one side the yellowed photos of the old cars and young men and on the other side the glossy photos of sleek new cars and older men. What the photos didn't show was how these men had drifted to selling shock absorbers or spark plugs as Sales Representatives, or gyppo used cars from a corner, or had died, in bed or in flaming wrecks on outlaw tracks—one by one. At the bottom was the smashed Novi that Fronty's boy had driven at Indy when the south corner had leaned out to meet him.

In the silence Mill turned and said: "Where's Long Tom?"

"Dead. Oh, I guess a year now."

Yes, he would be: a heart attack, no doubt. A warped valve no mechanic could ever reseat.

"But you remember Snuff," Fronty said, "he's still around. And Gee-Eye. You remember those guys?"

Yes, Mill remembered Snuff, a senile pensioner who believed all racing had ended with the board tracks. In the old days, when it had taken two men to handle a car, Snuff had ridden mechanic with some of the best. And Gee-Eye, who owned the diner down the street, bought at the end of

WW II with his mustering out pay. When Mill had hung around the garage while in high school those two guys, and Long Tom, had done a lot of bench racing.

This evidence of violence, a car through the fence, the towering column of acrid smoke, the catastrophe of a skidding death—whether on a wet-slick road or a dished-out bed—caused Mill to ask Fronty: "Does my brother Tonto ever come in here?" Mill had not seen his brother since his return, but he had found a cheap snub-nosed .38 pistol stuck under a pile of puchuko pants in the dresser, and he had heard his father's candid estimate of Tonto.

Fronty shook his head as he got two clean cups from the oil display case. "No, I don't think I know the boy. It's pretty quiet around here." He looked around the empty garage as if he had suddenly realized that the building *was* quiet.

Talk hesitated forward. Fronty chose his words the way he chose his friends, carefully, and Mill was hesitant, too, because he didn't want to sound stilted or condescending. So they talked about the one thing they both knew: cars.

The coffee pot perked its muffled report, and the bond between the crippled mechanic and the nervous, awkward boy was rebuilt. Because no one honked for service, nor pulled into the shadow of the pump island, time passed.

At one point Mill's roadster was mentioned, and Fronty asked whatever had happened to it. Mill said that it was outside, and it was out of gas.

Fronty raised himself in the chair to see beyond the misty windows—and then they were crossing the gravel, the boy walking, the man rolling his chair, to where the roadster angled at speed under the twin slash marks of the pumps. Fronty did one slow turn around the car, then unsnapped the hood latches and peered over the top of the side panel. The flathead V-8 was the same one that Fronty and Mill had assembled almost ten years ago.

"You know, this is a page from the past? There was a time, not so long ago, really, when this lot was filled with cars like this."

"I remember," Mill said. Times *had* changed, somewhat.

"But the old flathead is a good engine, and we built this one right."

"Not running so good today," Mill said. How could he ask Fronty for a few gallons of gas? He would pay him back when he got the Big Job.

"Well, it's been sitting for years. I know how that is," Fronty said. Mill wondered if the old man was joking about the wheel chair. More likely he was thinking about the two trailered race cars inside, where bearings were rusting into the crank journals.

"Put in some gas, and start it."

Fronty listened, eyes staring along the polished cooling fins and chrome acorn nuts. Finally, he told Mill to fold back the garage doors and to bring the car inside. There Fronty unzipped the Dzus fasteners on the hood and side panels, to expose the engine he had helped Mill build years before. He checked compression and retimed the ignition and cleaned the plugs. Mill passed tools, noting the compression meter's cracked face, the worn tune-up machine, and dull wrenches old, but still efficient, like the man.

It was valves, at the least. Working together, Mill and Fronty pulled off the heads; then they went deeper, to gut the block.

Throughout the long afternoon, the sun canted into the west, no one came in for repairs and only two cars bought gas, so they worked without interruption. It was dark when the engine was reassembled. Long ago, as if he knew the boy would someday come back, Fronty had bought two sets of piston rings for this engine.

Fronty adjusted the carb settings by ear and checked the timing again and then told Mill to fill the tank. With his ethyl.

But as the roadster idled at a smooth, vicious *scruumph scruumph* on the gravel apron, headlights aimed into the dark countryside, Fronty refused a ride. He must lock up, he said. Margie would expect him for dinner, anytime now.

Mill waved, stabbed the gas twice, and the rear tires broke traction slightly as he feathered the accelerator, holding power back until the rings were seated. And suddenly he realized two things: that he and the old man, occupied with the car, had not eaten a bite all day. Also, except for the two gas sales, there had not been any customers; Fronty had not earned coffee money.

The roadster chased its headlight beams into elusive darkness. This time it really ran—the complex valve and piston stroke was harmonized, each finger or fist of metal working with its activator. When Mill hit the pedal for an instant, the tach needle threatened to move past the redline, like a shade over the sun.

The only dissonance was the bell ping of spark knock.

Probably due to Fronty's gas, which was not endorsed by champions.

That he would work for Fronty was not discussed.

Mill was at the station the next morning when Fronty's old pickup crossed the gravel apron. Fronty eased his useless feet to the running board; from the bed he shook open the wheelchair with one hand, and all the time his eyes were on the boy. They said good morning; Fronty plugged in the coffeepot and Mill went to the workbench, where he gathered the filthy tools to soak in a pail of solvent. He had flopped only two box wrenches on the work bench, where they lay like shiny trout, when a car rattled over the gravel apron. The car was still rolling forward as the three boys jumped out to stand beside the hip-high roadster. Mill couldn't understand their reply to his question, so he filled their tank. With ethyl. He washed the windshield and when the boys slouched back they were thinking of the roadster, and did not even know they had paid.

Mill dropped the money in the empty cash box. "It is like a billboard, parked there."

Fronty nodded, although he didn't believe in advertising, or trading stamps, or company promotional gimmicks like free dishes, charm bracelets, stuffed animals. Good service and quality products sold gas, he always said. A man had to have integrity, even if he only ran a service station.

That he was hired at all was not discussed until the third day when at least part of the debt had been worked off. Fronty was reluctant to hire him; Mill should be out looking for the Big Job. He had an education, why would he want to waste his time in this remote service station, getting his hands dirty. It would only be for a few weeks, Mill argued, only until he could take the State Board Exam to become a licensed architect. Fronty couldn't argue that point, and gas sales *were* up—the roadster attracted every passing car.

Each morning Mill idled through the rows of tract houses, past the end of the busline, past the Galloping Goose tracks, past Inner's wrecking yard and The Curve, and into the country: the early morning speed run. To blow the carbon from the engine, he said; the exhaust note barking higher and higher against barns and scattering cows along fences. The streak of black hurtling over the road that dipped and heaved beneath it while Mill jotted notes on the dash-mounted clipboard. He raced through the morning air until, deep in the moist green landscape, the throttle was eased and speed passed him by.

He headed back to Fronty's, where he had cleaned every tool which hung in the neat rows on perforated wallboard. He had scrubbed the board floor with solvent, and cleared the debris from corners. But Fronty would not allow Mill to paint the station or the pickup truck company colors. Nor to accept trading stamps. The line must be drawn somewhere, he said.

Why had he returned home? He had returned home to avoid complexities, he told himself; he wanted to sink

9

slowly into the simple past. Because he didn't want to answer questions about the Big Job, Mill stayed at the garage during the day, and sometimes it was ten before he walked into his parents' empty front room, into the TV's acetylene light. He had spent five years becoming an architect, and how could he expect them to understand *why* he had taken a job in Fronty's run-down, edge-of-the-city service station? They expected so much more.

"—always knew I had it here," his father had said that first night at dinner, pointing at a place just above where the hard-hat made a permanent crease in his hair. The food came by: hamburger with wheat bran, mashed potatoes, white relief gravy, and home-canned crimson carrots. Beneath the table and to the four walls linoleum stretched like an old gray rhinoceros hide. The wallpaper, the tooth-scraped silverware, the chipped plates were familiar patterns, and in some ways it seemed as if he had never left home at all. Yet in the awkward silence he did not feel familiar. He looked at his mother, his sister Audrey, at Granny mouthing her baby food, and he seemed to see strangers—like Loaner's Corners, like the entire city, they had changed.

"—and here," his father said, clenching his fist. "With an education I could've done anything."

"Mill... Mill," Granny sang at the ceiling light; she was almost eighty, and he was certain that she did not remember him. "Mill," she snapped, staring at where the tic in his left cheek throbbed. "Got an education. They can't take that away from you."

"That's right, Granny," Mill said, as the throb jerked his mouth into a smile. Whenever he realized how much that scrap of paper meant to his family, he felt as though he had betrayed them, and for a quick moment he told himself that he *would* find a good job, that he *would* be successful.

But after supper he and his father went into the front room and there on the coffee table were two books that caused him to renounce his good intentions: his mother's heavy Bible, well-thumbed, and beside it his father's scrapbook. Without opening the cover Mill knew that every page contained scraps of dreams cut from popular magazines: INVESTIGATE ACCIDENTS. Earn $750 to $1,000 monthly. No college necessary. Learn Pulp and Papermaking Industry at home, men needed for this High Paying field. HOME MAIL-ORDER BUSINESS, simple, enjoyable. Detective Profession. Easy home study plan. Lapel pin. Earn CASH clipping local papers.

His father leveled two glasses of wine, toasted Mill's future, and turned on the TV—because he wanted to be kept informed. "Beginning tomorrow I shall inquire about a situation for you." He assured Mill he was on speaking terms with many architects, and he would inquire about openings. Only in the finest firms, you understand. Although, ahhhhh, frankly, there was the private opinion that he could do the layout work better than most desk jockeys. You understand? Mill didn't doubt that his father could do the architect's work; he wasn't dumb and he worked hard—but none of his dreams had come true, to date.

The tic grew under the skin of his cheek, and Mill pressed against it with a thumb. "Don't try too hard at first. There's the State Exam."

"The State Exam..." His father took a long drink and looked at his own shoe in a profound way. "I have a couple of friends in the State Highway Commission." He winked, and told Mill that it was perfectly all right; it was not at all unusual. How did the boy suppose everyone got their relatives on Civil Service payrolls?

Mill wanted to ask about Tonto, his brother, but soon his father's chin slumped to his chest in final, total fatigue—it had been a hard day. Mill went to the front door and looked at the summer night through the screen. No sign of Tonto, who had not come home for dinner. Again he thought of the .38 pistol he had found an hour earlier under a pile of black puchuko pants in his brother's room, and he knew what he had to do: find Tonto.

He walked through the neighborhood, and even in the dark he could sense the familiar: paint peeled from houses, sagging porches, the debris of yards, the abandoned cars with four flat tires. There was a kind of suspended helplessness in the direction these curving lines took–of living from payday to payday. Then he was on Foster Road, and approaching Loaner's Corners. The intersection was an island of small shops, most built fifty years before when Loaner's Corner was a farmer's market; only the Rexall Drug, remodeled in rectangles of glass and sandstone veneer, seemed newer than World War II. Most of the other stores had become industrial centers: Goodwill Industries, Union Gospel Mission Industries, Salvation Army and St. Vincent de Paul Industries. The rest–the taverns and second hand shops–waited stoically for Urban Renewal.

Grogan's hadn't changed; thick talk and smoke, beer and brine, dark worn wood, frayed deer heads, the pool table's felt in tatters. Even the hierarchy of the place was unchanged: paying customers at the bar, those nursing a glass in the middle of the room, and, against the far wall, sat the old men who spent their shadowy lives here.

Mill bought a beer and listened to a man with a railroad hat who was talking to Grogan and an old Legionnaire: "I was all set to go to Texas. On a lawsuit. Martin comes to me and says, 'Did you inspect car so and so on such and such a day on a certain train?'

" 'I don't remember,' I says.

" 'Well,' he says, 'were there any cars of blank blank,' and he names a train.

" 'I have no idea,' I says.

" 'Well, was it light or dark at the time?' he asks.

" 'Could not say,' I says. And I ask him why he's asking.
" 'A man in Texas put his foot through the hole in a car

floor and was damn neared killed. Was that hole there when you inspected those cars?'

" 'Naw,' I tell him, 'that car was in perfect shape.' " The three men guffawed, clawing the air; Grogan wiped down the bar and asked, "That trip would have been all expense paid, wouldn't it?"

"Oh shit yes," the railroad man laughed.

A lemon-colored man followed his beer down the bar.

"That reminds me of the time I was overseeing the loading of some lumber down at the dock. I fool around with lumber from time to time, y'know. Get tired of pushing that desk around..."

Mill picked up his change and went to the sidewalk; he did not want to hear any more sweet dreams of laborers—his father's were enough.

He looked through the window of The Shack, where dancers bopped to the jukebox, but he didn't see Tonto. Two boys braced the doorway; one mouthed a cigarette and the other snapped his fingers as Mill's heel hit the walk. "Heay man. You dropped something."

Startled by the flat hardness of the voice Mill turned to the boys who stood with thumbs cocked in low, tight black pants.

"Heay man. Pick it up. Before you bleed to death."

They rocked with laughter as Mill, dull with surprise, was anchored to the sidewalk. The two boys convulsed with laughter at the old joke, and began a tight, savage dance in the doorway.

Mill's fists clenched as the tic warped the left side of his face, pulling his lips into a foolish smile; he turned and walked urgently past the Goodwill Industries, the St. Vincent de Paul, the rummage stores, past all the accumulated junk, and followed Foster Road toward where the city was couched in reflected light. Somewhere a motorcycle barked its feverish tempo through the gears, the exhaust note rising and falling with the precision of a knife. A train whistle sounded at the edge of the world, perverse in its connotations of travel. Distant, isolated noises in a huge silent world.

He came to where Foster crossed Highway 82, and saw the lights of Hubert's (Open All Nite) Drive Inn; crossing the highway he was at the center line when he saw the group of boys in the parking lot, primer gray in the dark. Mill braked to a stop as speeding cars swerved, honked, blinded him with their chrome-smooth passage. But he could not move: the instinctual, metallic fear the gang generated was greater than the danger of spinning tires, unyielding fenders, and the razor edges of bumpers.

Then, as Mill straddled the yellow lines, he saw the girl. She was a head taller than any of the boys, standing high as she worked on the pavement to the screech-saw music from a car radio. The girl and a dwarfed boy moved like traffic dancers—bodies contorted in kinky, erratic bends until a spasm forced the hips in and bellies skidded together, and always their arms beat at the night.

Mill woke up, and tasted fear. Keeping his eyes on the dancers he felt his way to the curb and safety; spying over a car's hood he saw the girl's partner move away into the finger-snapping circle and another boy move in. Mill's throat locked in surprise: there was something too familiar about the high, starved cheeks, the sharply angular nose, the extended neck. It was like seeing a younger photo of himself, and he realized *this must be Tonto* who now touched bellies with the tall girl while all the traffic in the world rushed past oblivious to the blasting radio, the grinding hips, waving arms, and sleek hard butts.

Perhaps it was the traffic dancers viewed between flashing cars, or the thought of that snub-nosed .38 pistol in his brother's drawer, or the picture of his father slumped in the chair facing the TV's brilliant light that urged him a couple of days later to take that job at Fronty's—it was the only possible escape from the web of complexities that threatened already to draw him in.

The high summer grass buzzed with heat and insects, like the angry snarl of the chain-saw high on the mountain. The summer heat buzzed into shimmering waves, while in the cool dark cave Mill passed another day doing the reasonable, methodical repair work, or listening to the rambling talk of Snuff Martindale, as the old man's mind went into a four wheel drift.

"Kids nowadays can't drive a peg in a pig's ass."

The old men sat in the sun beside the battered Coke machine. Fronty smiled as Snuff ranted: "She's all a straight line, the drag."

"And on the track," Mill shouted from the darkness, "on the track she's one big left turn."

Snuff beat the dirt with his cane—for him racing had ended when they took out the riding mechanic. But he had been one of the best, at a time when tires could split off wooden rims and the cars had almost no brakes at all. It was Snuff who had taught Fronty about engines, and Fronty taught Mill; from master to apprentice knowledge was passed down, kept alive.

"Kids can't drive a peg..."

Wheels rattled across the gravel. Mill wiped his hands as a twenty foot gold convertible rolled in with a cloud of dust. They did not often get customers like this and it all looked like money, so Mill was on the island when the girl said: "Fill 'er up, buddy."

Mill stuck the nozzle in the filler neck and went forward for the windshield; under his fingers he could feel the insects, all totaled on the glass, and keeping his head back he could see the woman's legs tapering to meet the pedals—the skirt was pulled above the knees, the way women drivers will do. He gave each headlight a swipe and was on the passenger side glass when the man pointed: a yellowish hump of insect Mill had missed. Inside the glass the fat finger with the bulging ring withdrew to wipe the sweat from the man's mustache.

Mill got to the rear just in time to catch the pump nozzle, which did not have an automatic shutoff. The woman's face was a dusty tan except for the peeling red nose, and beyond it was the landscape of plush red leather. It was a composition of beauty and money, of debutantes and private swimming pools.

"Check your water and oil, ma'm?"

She hesitated. As Mill wondered was she reading something into his suggestion—thinking, perhaps, of phallic dipsticks—she rubbed that polished, peeling nose and said: "No, s'all right."

"Then that's twelve twenty-six."

Again she hesitated. When he expected possibly a credit request ('Cash Only,' the mauve and gilt rimmed sign in Fronty's office read. 'Credit Makes Enemies, Let's Be Friends'), or a credit card (Fronty didn't believe in them—money by proxy), she had the money out the window.

"C'mon, Joanie," the man said. "Let's go."

"What would it cost?" she asked. "If it were for sale?" Her eyes remained on the roadster, that black and chrome forward slanting segment of steel, tucked between four naked tires, which sat on this edge-of-the-world dilapidated station.

The passenger grunted when Mill said: "It's not for sale, really." Not even today, when he was absolutely broke—like Fronty, he too wished to live in the past.

As he turned back tires fizzled twin paths of gravel, which rattled off the roof and tin oil signs, and Mill went into the office to the old men, feeling he had lost some kind of wealth he never actually had.

If it were for sale…But, it is not.

He dropped the money into Fronty's cash box and locked the lid. Across the smear of dark floor and the grease pit's crater, and beyond the rhythm of wrenches—box and open end, crescent and spanner, stillson and ratchet, aligned by type and length on the perforated wallboard—were the trailered midget racers, idle and aging. He dropped into the swivel chair and cocked his feet on the roll-top desk, where he could see the wall of photographs.

"Could you make money with them, Fronty?"

Always the winner's purse was divided many ways, and the machine got the biggest slice: tires sheared of tread, an overheated engine, a rod spinning anarchy through the wall of a special block. Or a badly judged comer, a sweeping slide, and the fence.

"I mean big money," Mill said, thinking of the twenty foot gold convertible. For Mill had decided he would like to be substantial in the *kind* of work he preferred.

"Some have," Fronty said, his voice drifting off, his eyes seeing sights other than the room. "Indianapolis, of course, the big one. And the Grand Pree races..."

Mill considered this, and the two trailered race cars, and the pictures on the wall, where a man risked his life for no more than a trophy, and he realized again why they had never had any money: They raced because they loved speed, and fine machinery, and the anarchy of a high winding engine, and whatever else it is that makes a man race. They raced to risk their lives wheel to wheel at a hundred mph plus, or to simply ruin their health in the noxious fumes of alcohol and nitro fuels, until they coughed blood—like Tazio Nuvolari, who was the greatest of them all.

Across the countryside the sun canted up, the prolepsis of another hot day. Mill shook off any dream of money and went outside to fill the blank spaces on the oil display rack. Then he began to assemble a farmer's rototiller and had it together when the sun and his belly cried lunchtime.

17

Chapter 2

Across from the unmarked Curve was the wrecking yard, and on the sprawling, leaning wood fence, a wreck in its own buckled way, were the faded circus letters: INNER MCMAHON Prop. The location was a natural: the trolley crossing or the blind curve caught the unwary motorist, and the drunk did not really have a chance. Under the Curve, like a net, was the cornfield, also owned by Inner.

At Inner's the past swept Mill back. To face the leaning fence was to face a thousand hubcap moons, a thousand rusty eyes. Inside, he picked up the axle, swung it against the suspended driveline and steel forged steel. Concentric sound waves lapped the contorted shattered car forms, examples of death. Row after row of battered, humped tops and sightless windshields, cars parked without priority: the older rusted at the rear, waiting until they would become a foundation for a supermarket.

There was only one new car on the lot: an Alpha Romeo coupe near the gate, top torn back as one might open a can.

Mill was struck by the static quality of the yard: things did not change here, the broken chassis and flat tires did not go anywhere. The progressive wrecking yards removed any part of a shattered car that could be resold for profit. They racked and binned the parts and kept inventory. The body steel, which was nearly worthless and occupied taxable land, was sent to the scrap yard, where a press diminished a full size sedan to a bale no larger than a decent tombstone.

He banged the bars again, as the man came from the little room behind the office *(We aim to please...)*, yanking on his belt, struggling with his fly *(... so please to aim)*. Inner's mouth was open but he suppressed the angry blind shout when he saw Mill. He pitched forward in surprise, then leaned back on his cane, an old touring car top bow trimmed down.

Mill found the wrecker unchanged: oh, perhaps a few less teeth sucked behind the wet, troll lips, and the old man was angled forward a bit, as if assuming a pose of speed. But the stubborn strength was still there, seen in the arms, where the tattooed skin was color faded under dust, and at the sides of his neck, and in the way he stood with his feet jacked apart.

The long second passed.

"–a sorry sonvabitch," Inner said, lips drawn past the spoked wheel of teeth. "It is, yessir, Mill Sederstrom. Fat from collich and you didn't forget old Mr. McMahon." Inner swayed, then swept the quilted greasy skull cap off and led the way into the cave that was his office. A blackness descended, and Mill could scarcely see the cane, pointing at the wall.

"For guests of honor."

It was A-grade leather, the back seat from some elegant sedan. Mill accepted this shelter in the tailpipe jungle, the forest of dangling axles, the foliage of fan belts and tubes hung like nooses. Every inch was a confusion of machinery. The nooks and bins and barrels, pistons and bearings and rods and gears and parts unknown even to their owner—and all obsolete.

Inner pointed down his finger, then erected it.

"Up yours, m'boy, for ever coming back. The big city's where a man makes his dough. Don't they teach you kids that in collich?" He reached into the three legged safe near his foot and the green pint bottle his hand came out with was held to the light. "To peace and prosperity," he said, pouring the liquid into grease-rimmed piston cups, "or a prosperous piece."

It was *Greeneye,* the go ahead. Homecut, and as it ran like little knives Mill truly believed the accusation of five year old anti-freeze, aged in copper radiator tubes and seasoned with rust. The wrecker drank, brushed the runoff into the black skid marks of whiskers, and quickly reached down to rub his ponderous belly.

"Well," Mill said, looking around the cave, where the sweet, thick smell of bearing grease hung in the air like honey, "business hasn't changed."

"It will," Inner said, now rubbing his hands together in another kind of anticipation. "Yessir, I need that card and index system. Do want to get organized, to clear out the slow movers." He surveyed his crop of parts and Mill, who had heard this dream before, who could imagine how meager the harvest would be, let his eyes focus on the fastback Alpha Romeo coupe near the gate.

Inner's finger searched the high-pocket of his overalls, drew out a smashed pack, and shook three half-cigarettes to the counter. He lit one and as the match flared Mill waited for the explosion of Greeneye. "Got to get modern."

"I heard that ten years ago," Mill said, remembering when he was a kid standing around the yard on Saturday afternoons, wiping his nose on his sleeve and dreaming of fast, cutdown cars. And even earlier than that, when he had ridden his bicycle this way and had stood on the seat to see his reflection in the lowest hubcap on the board fence, which in those days was just beginning to warp. *"And nothing has changed.* Except for the Alpha coupe, and that doesn't belong."

Through the slanted outline of the door the coupe was hunched forward. Weeds poked from fender wells, to root the car to earth, and an inch of mud coated the left side: already the yard claimed the car, pulling it hubcap high into the ground.

"Was a stranger passing through who'd had a few too many, no doubt. Was unfamiliar with The Curve and went into the cornfield, which I own. The feller didn't have a chance, as you can see; I got it from the insurance boys, for a song."

Now, Mill supposed, Inner was thinking of sports car parts exclusively. A nicer bunch of people to deal with. Class. Cigars. Ascots and thin mustaches.

Mill looked from the car to the wrecker, and asked Inner whether he knew Tonto—that had been his main reason for coming to the wrecker's yard.

"Tonto? Yeah, I know him. He comes in once in a while."

Mill was surprised, and tried to imagine his little brother standing among the junk that rusted into pools. "How long since you saw him?"

"Maybe a month," Inner said. "The truth is I don't think he knows his pee-er from a piston. Unlike his brother. Remember that jalopy you had, that old tin bucket you was always working on?"

"I still have it," Mill said.

"You still got it?" Inner roared, as if he didn't live in the past. "Why, then you've owned that car fifteen years."

"Ten," Mill said, getting up from the A-grade leather seat, going to the door to survey the rusting landscape.

"Why," Inner screamed, "you ain't going to look for the Big Job in that bucket of bolts. Who d'you think'll hire you for a Position when you drive up in hell on wheels?"

To bait the wrecker, Mill said, "How's Fronty Merrimac?"

Inner's face twisted into a series of wrinkles, a washboard road, before he turned and spit into the packed ground.

"Still pressing, I suppose. I haven't walked around that Curve for thirty years. And I never will. You know that. I wouldn't give the old coot a shove off the tracks if his chair was smack square in front of the Galloping Goose, if it was still running. Hell, you know that."

Mill knew, which was why he baited the wrecker. Four country blocks apart for thirty years and enemies for most of that. Old men who had worked together on cars no longer manufactured—Durant and Paige and Willys-Knights and Apperson—and now cleared from the road. Old men angry over something they probably couldn't remember.

"What was the trouble?" Mill asked, with mock seriousness. The cause of their fight was never discussed.

"A head hard as this fender," Inner swung an axle at the metal and it sounded back, striking the curtain of tailpipes, which reverberated like small bells; the ring of metal echoed within the building, poured from the open door to lap each shattered, contorted wreck, humped to its final end. Some things had not changed for thirty years.

Other things *had* changed after only a few years. Mill had been home almost two weeks before he met Tonto. He was up before the rest of the family, anxious to be gone so that he wouldn't have to answer their questions about why he was working at Fronty's. He was shaving, and as the faucets cleared air, back-fired, as pipes rattled all through the house Mill heard a step in the hallway. The door flew open, and Mill jumped, the razor held away from his face.

There was Tonto: no longer an eleven year old kid, his face assumed a mechanical rigidity and his body was like a tensionless spring. He ignored Mill's greeting and the outstretched hand; after a long silence, as the two brothers observed one another, he said: "Man, how come you're back?"

"I don't get you?"

"Why, like you were real gone, man. Y'know?"

Mill looked at his own bare feet and withdrew his hand.

He was afraid he might laugh--or perhaps simply afraid. Tonto's narrowed eyes and grotesque hair, swept into long, slick fenders over the ears and combed back to a V, inspired the menacing fear of movie gangs. Mill recalled the revolver buried under the stack of freshly ironed puchuko pants, and saw again the savage night dance in Hubert's (Open All Nite) Drive-Inn parking lot, where anarchy rocked to a full race car radio. When he looked up, Tonto was gone.

Mill washed off his razor and sat on the toilet lid to pull on his shoes; one shoe was on and tied when Tonto reappeared.

"Oh yes. I mean Daddy-O has been making big promises. For *five lousy years*. But you come home and I have to sleep on that cruddy davenport. That wasn't the scene I expected. I mean, like *that's* success?"

Tonto fired the words in hate and then rested against the narrow doorway like a punch-drunk fighter, chin riding the ridge of his collar-bone, head ducked to reveal each hair carefully combed into a slick wave. The sleeves of his T-shirt were rolled to the shoulder, where slim arms hung loose to thumbs hitched in Tonto's back pockets. Then, although the boy seemed to have no energy, he curled his lip and moved quickly away.

Well crissakes, Mill mumbled, shoving on his other shoe, willing to be down the road, to forget Tonto and home and Loaner's Corner, and, yes, even Fronty's.

"I mean," Tonto said, immediately reappearing, "you have learned everything. *In five years.* Indeedy."

"Knock that shit off—what is it, airplane dope?"

"Airplane dope, that's rich. Man, you are behind the times. You're way out there, somewhere," Tonto said, his slack hand fanning the breeze, and then he turned and bounced lightly down the stairs with a taut, primitive grace. From the curb came the scream of tires, and through the window Mill saw the '49 Ford slouch away, a tailpipe striking sparks as it hit the pavement.

As he went back to his room he heard the sound of slow shuffling on the stairs, as his mother led Granny toward the kitchen. The old woman glanced at Mill, and mumbled: *Education... can't take away, Education... can't take,* as if she was reminding herself who Mill was, or daring *them* to try, or was by this ritual somehow insuring the family's wealth.

Chapter 3

Early Sunday morning Mill slipped neat, starch-stiff coveralls over his underwear—the roadster was tuned, and he wanted to see what she would do, against the clocks. Even if the drag was all a straight line, where a kid did not need to know enough to drive a peg in a pig's ass, the small ad he had seen on Wednesday said each class winner would receive a hundred dollar bond. For the fastest time of the day there was five hundred dollars. He had to begin somewhere, and the roadster was tuned.

The airport was ten miles south of town in a dished pocket of the valley. A small private field, the runway had been extended far into the wheat field to allow the cars to accelerate from a standing start and hurtle toward the timing clocks exactly a quarter mile away.

It was seven years since Mill had raced there.

In those days he had gone with friends, the pack of hip high roadsters and chopped coupes screaming balls-out through the clear silver dawn. They fought the morning's damp chill with army surplus tanker jackets and Thermos bottles of coffee; later, when the sun rocked against its apogee, they fought heat with Cokes cooled under the CO_2 fire extinguisher. And they returned at dusk with a trophy or a busted engine—happy, tired, young.

Today he went it alone.

The roadster churned the flat, blank asphalt away from the city; on either side the country broadened into wide fields, toward the dorsal fins of mountains which defined the horizon—to the right the Coast Range, to the left the Cascades. Mill was funneled down the valley floor until he saw the parking area in the distance, a speckled field of color, chrome, and reflected glass. The billboard grew to meet him, the two cars charging forever the suspended checkered flag:

Drag Racing at Hotten's
Every Other Sun.
& bring the kiddies.

Throttling back Mill followed the arrow down a thin dirt road, into the drifting dust of the red pickup and trailer. The cool breeze of motion gone, he realized it would be hot, this day. The golden fields were like mirrors reflecting the sun.

Over the sound of his engine he heard another, and looked into the crystalline, cloudless sky. A silver bi-plane, with red sunbursts along the wings, swept over the fields and began a long, slow climb.

Mill pulled into the line at the Competitors' Gate, and marveled at the changes: seven years ago hardly anyone had towed his car out, nor had there been a long line of factory sedans, ready to race right off the dealer's showroom floor, nor had there been so many spectators. Now even the TV cameras were interested in drag racing and, unlike Fronty's midget racing circles, it had prospered into an Industry.

Overhead the bi-plane reached the sun and hung suspended, a narrow strip of aluminum. Balanced in space the plane stalled, and slowly, gracefully fell on one wing, sliding toward the golden fields. Nose heavy, when it dropped straight the dead propeller spun, the engine caught and, screaming its optimum, raced the plane earthward in a steep dive. Halfway between the sun and earth white smoke jetted from the exhaust, tracing the plane's passage through the cloudless sky. Mill sighted ahead of the plane at the projected point of impact, where men were running for cover. Under his coveralls he felt a chill: instinctually he knew that if the plane's flight could not be halted, the crash, like an embarrassing moment, should not be seen. Down the plane plunged, as if emerging from the past, and when only fifty feet remained between the flimsy arrangement of fabric and wire and the ultimate, destructive earth, the nose lifted, the smoke broke off, and the plane's staccato power roared overhead. Above the cockpit Mill could see the pilot's chamois flying cap and white scarf.

Today, Mill suddenly realized, was July the Fourth–Independence Day. It was Hotten's way of giving the crowd its money's worth.

A boy Tonto's age came down the line handing out slips of paper. At Mill's door his hand remained for a long second on the burnished metal, and Mill recognized the kid's bright eyes and cockeyed grin. When the boy asked what'll she do? Mill shrugged: he did not know.

The paper was both entry form and release, severing Hotten from any legal responsibility in case of accident. A second boy took the paper and Mill's five dollars, and the roadster surged past the bushes into the pit area.

Mill heard the Dragster on the line.

He pulled into the slot beside the big red pickup. His engine cut, Mill heard the terrible swelling of open exhaust stacks as the Dragster on the line revved for the start. Standing on the roadster's seat he could not see the starting light nor the car, but he felt the air tremble over the roofs of reflected sunlight as the Dragster suddenly burst out of its own smoke, tires burning the entire quarter-mile until the bright drag chute billowed out behind. Smoke drifted off the strip, and the air was still except for the muted explosion of fire crackers.

A hunnert ninety-three point fifty-four on that last run folks, e. t. was eight-fourteen. An' let's givem a big hand folks...

Mill jumped from the roadster, amazed that any car could hit almost two-hundred mph in the space of five city blocks and a deep breath. He walked toward the starting line, into the heat of engines and sun. In the pit area men swarmed over gleaming, precise machines; the sun blazed from chrome upswept exhaust stacks, magnesium wheels, and metallic paint.

On the line Wheelie Walters from Salem charges the C/FD record in a Dodge... Waitaminute! There was some difficulty–a plane wants to land–

On the line the Dodge engine rose and fell as the temperature approached boiling. Far back in the pits someone yelled: *Frig the gawdamn plane, shoot it down!* A beer bottle arced across the sky.

But when the bi-plane glided in from above the trees, the propeller spinning lazily, it made no pretense of landing: as it hovered overhead an arm reached from the cockpit and the gloved fist opened—the five pound bag of flour tumbled through space into the center of the bull's eye spray-painted on the ground.

Even before the plane roared off into a barrel-roll toward the sun, the announcer chuckled: *Okee Wheelie she's your show on the ground...*

In the short second before the Christmas tree lights spurted Go, Mill saw the Dodge sedan levitate under torque, and the hood lift toward the fading plane. The pavement shook under the assault of eight down-turned exhaust megaphones. Mill noticed the huge rear slicks, the heavy, braced roll bar under the roof, the driver's asbestos fire suit and face mask; then the lights flashed Go and the big Dodge sedan was gone: slicks bit into asphalt, churning solid smoke and the front tires jumped five feet off the ground. For part of a second the car was airborne, as if caught in an attitude of surprise; when smoke poured from the rear fender wells the engine screamed across the hard pavement; the shift to second, front wheels touching quickly and bouncing again into the air and somewhere along the horizon of tire smoke and shimmering heat Mill heard another shift and saw the crimson parachute stream out and snap open, a brilliant red circle swirling into the exhaust staccato.

She was not a track record folks, the announcer was saying, as Mill shook off surprise: his fists clenched tightly and he felt the tic creep far beneath his cheek. *Not a record but a good show...*

Seven years ago, he thought, a full-out, fuel burning rail had *almost* turned a hundred and forty-four in the quarter, or a high-boy competition roadster *might* go that fast, given five

27

miles of Bonneville salt, but this was a passenger car, a family sedan, with four doors, a radio and heater.

Let's give Wheelie a nice hand folks...

Mill walked to his car, the burst of applause at his back as the Dodge coasted along the return strip.

The two men from the Dragster were hovering about its engine, and as Mill began to detach the headlights from his roadster one man said: "Sonny, what kind of engine you got there?"

Mill saw their grinning faces reflected in the chrome, saw the same cockeyed grins the kid at the gate had worn and now he realized that even the kid had known when he had asked: What'll she do?

"Oh, look, Spud, those jugs are Strombergs."

"Well, you're right, Chub, and it says Offenhauser on the heads. Why I bet this's a real Offy engine."

"Never knowed they made a V-8," Spud said, and the two men stumbled back to their Dragster, laughing, as Mill began to tighten the headlight nut. He had the hubcaps back on and the tool box in the trunk when four identical men stepped onto the grass. Their white shirts and pith helmets said TECH COMMITTEE. All wore white pants and white sneakers and sunglasses.

The one with the clip-board looked over the roadster and said: "Thinking of racing?"

"I was."

"Times have changed, and you need to make some changes. First of all you need a hood," he said. "And a regulation size roll bar, and a full scatter shield, and safety-hubs on the rear, and a fire extinguisher, and..."

They gave him a rule book and told him to study it.

Times had changed, they said. As he pulled out of the pits toward the pay shack he saw four bottles of beer lifted from the cooler in the red pickup truck bed, and heard the loud laughter.

An Offen-hauser, for sure...

At the pay shack the boy had to make a phone call: Hotten did not often refund the money. There was some trouble with the phone and then with Hotten, and Mill turned toward the strip, where an engine barked. High overhead, the bi-plane glinted against the cloudless sky. Mill saw a figure crawl along a lower wing, a spider in a web of struts and wires; the figure dropped off, tumbling, swimming through blue space toward the ground. Mill was beyond surprise, but his cheek trembled until the sky-diver's chute snapped open a scant two hundred feet from the golden fields.

Then Mill saw the poster: *Ten Thousand,* it said.

Finally the boy hung up the receiver and gave Mill two fifty: Hotten would break an old rule and go half-way. Mill didn't argue—he took the money and tires spun across the grass, past the grinning boy who looked like Tonto, and at the dirt road Mill tromped the gas to the floor, leaving a dense brown cloud of dust in his wake, to funnel into the air and drift slowly back on the spectators: they would know he had been here.

But there had been time, while the boy picked his nose and waited for Hotten's decision, for Mill to slide off the hot leather seat and rip from the pay shack's wall the crisp, slick poster: *GRAND PRIX Ten Thousand...* To fold the poster into a neat square and shove it into his coveralls, where it burned against his ribs like a prophecy.

At dusk Mill swung the wheel in a short arc and crossed the littered parking lot of Hubert's (Open All Nite) Drive-Inn; he flipped off the ignition and left his lights on until the girl came out to take his order. He noticed her tight, white blouse, and the crotch-bound black slacks shiny in his lights: she is a cute kid, he thinks. But now he only wanted something to eat: all afternoon he had been drinking at Grogan's, his ears assailed by the flat crack of pool balls, the ripping of cloth as a cue swerved out of control, the lapping waves of booze talk. On the jukebox it was Country &

Western, wailing sad: lost girls, lost homes, lost buddies. He had sat all afternoon against the wall, wondering why he'd come back home, and suddenly aware that he would end up not like Fronty but like one of the old men in Grogan's, against the wall of life. Years of Grogan's brine, the foam dissolving his bones until he wouldn't be able to hold a pool cue firmly; then sitting, fingering his social security check across the bar dime by dime while the sad cowboy songs go around and around and Loaner's Corner collapses, the walls tumbling over his dull snow white head, squeezing his spongy brine-softened brain.

His eyes followed the car-hop to the swinging door and, in the shadows beside the building, he saw the knot of kids built around the motorcycle. With them was one girl taller even than the boy dressed in black cycle leathers.

Suddenly aware of where he was, Mill searched the other cars on the parking looking for Tonto.

His order came, and the hamburger was swimming in exactly the amount of grease he had expected. He ate quickly, intently, and was at first unaware of the Police Ford that cruised slowly across the littered lot and stopped before the roadster. The men studied the cut-down car in an official way, in case they might see it sometime screaming full-bore through dark, public streets. The kids turned their leather-jacketed backs to the headlights, and someone yelled: *What are cheap pennies made of?* And a voice replied: *Dirty copper!*

Other cars drove through but Mill didn't see Tonto's battered sedan. He finished his second hamburger and was fishing out the money when he saw the girl swing through the doorway, dancing toward the cycle's chrome gas tank. In shadows there was a flash of white thigh as her leg traveled in a piston stroke and an engine cracked the night. The machine lunged from the shadows and with the precision of chrome glided to the far end of the parking lot.

Mill flipped on his headlights as the other light struck him. From the far end of the lot the cycle accelerated straight toward the roadster, the headlight spreading from a dime in a tunnel to searchlight intensity.

Ten feet away the exhaust backed off, the headlight swerved, and Mill breathed deeply. The machine glanced into the shadows, then swerved back to the island of light. The girl's skirt was tucked beneath her; a long, white leg dropped to the pavement and slowly the cycle orbited the roadster, circling tighter and tighter until the arched handlebars nearly clipped the car.

The cycle braked, dipped. The girl hit the kill button and at the final *whump-whump* the cycle rocked on its jiffy stand.

The car-hop took Mill's money and tray, while on the other side the girl slid in. "Any room, man?"

Her skirt draped far above the white knees, her blouse was open at the throat by two buttons too many and below that she was full and soft. Her long fingers played along the gear shift, examining that long chrome rod. "Nice wheels," she said. "I'm Eddie."

Eddie, he thought—it would be something like Eddie, or Billie, or Joe. Something hard. In his headlights he saw the faces at the window. "Do you entertain nightly for them?"

"You got it wrong, man—like they entertain for me. It's crazy, you know?"

Mill figured he did know. He was about to ask whether she knew Tonto when light spread from the rectangle of the open door: there were five boys, led by the one encased in sleek cycle leathers.

"Roll, man, unless you can handle it."

There was no fear in her voice, only the flat, taut hardness of suppressed excitement. Mill turned the key and moved the gear shift into low. Inside, someone dropped money into the jukebox and the parking lot was flooded with nervous, erratic music. Mill was surprised to find his cheek calm, the tic gone.

The five moved into a circle, bopping to the sound of the heavy guitar. The motorcycle boy stood a foot from

Mill's door, thumping a gloved fist into the palm of the other.

"Cool it, Gus," Eddie said. "He's taking me for a ride."

"Oh indeedy," Gus said, "and what else do you do?"

"Anybody I can," Mill said. "Anybody worth the trouble."

Laughter stopped as two boys grabbed the back of the roadster and rocked it violently. Mill reached for the door handle, then for the starter button. "Knock it off," he said.

"Willingly." Gus stepped forward, arm cocked; his fist hit empty air as the roadster jerked, tires spinning, and the two boys behind were yanked a few feet and flipped away.

At the street, Mill said: "Get out!"

"Better roll, man," Eddie said, laughing as she slid down on the seat, arms over her head.

Above the screaming jukebox Mill heard feet running and he pulled into the street; a shadow threw something that whined overhead and past, as Mill put the gas to the floor.

He wound the engine tight in low gear, and shifted quickly to second.

No one followed them, nor did he drop Eddie off at the next intersection: the hell with it, he thought, it had been a hard day. He ignored her demand that they race every car that pulled hubcap to hubcap beside them—he drove slowly and where the red warning lights of the radio towers blinked he turned left, toward Mt. Scott. The road swept upward, curved to the very top, to the two radio towers, and just past their concrete feet he killed the engine.

"The Point," Eddie said. "How romantic. Why, you *are* interested in us kids." She opened her door and began to walk.

The Point was a promontory, barren except for the single huge Douglas fir whose roots held the jutting land to the mountain; where the grass ended was a drop of fifty feet, and far below that the city stretched on all sides into darkness. Toward The Point Eddie ran, legs flashing. Then like a child she pitched forward to her hands: Mill saw the two spire-like legs balanced white against darkness as the skirt dropped over her face, and although he felt a lunge of excitement in his chest all he could say was, "Watch out for broken glass."

"O Daddy," Eddie said, laughing, dropping to her feet with a liquid motion, "they do break them, don't they? Those damn kids."

"I meant, be careful."

"Maybe I don't want to be careful," she said, and poised above the city she took his arm. Against him he felt softness and warmth, and it was easy to remember all the other times he had ever been at The Point—those nights when time stretched on and the clock on the newspaper tower seemed to stop.

Her arm moved around his waist and she was half-turned toward him, pulling him down beside her on the grass that smelled like damp, black leather.

Under The Point the town faded into a night as taut as a trampoline-the thousand lights were reflected as points overhead. To the west, from Oaks Park a barrage of rockets traced skyward, burst, and fell in fading embers; seconds later the explosions tumbled to their ears.

His cigarette curved away into space, a line of fire etched into the night, and his mouth found hers—he was amazed that her full lips were at the same time very soft and very hard, like the delicate tongue that searched his mouth. She rolled beneath him, her long thighs moving, and grasped his hand to place on her breast—which instantly hardened. Under pressure he broke the long kiss and raised his head—beneath him her hair fanned over the grass, her smile was urgent, and where the blouse had fallen away her skin was whiter than the bra strap. She moaned and pulled him down again, her lips opened against his, her hard hips driving upward.

Below them, in every sad house, accounts were being settled; paychecks were balanced against the eternal bills and visits to the finance company. For those people the clock on the *Journal* tower raced on, while they parked their lives before the TV's white glare.

A hand ran along his arm and around his neck while the other searched his front pocket.

Across the city fireworks were exploding in dazzling pyrotechnics, and Mill told himself he was an Independent, he was neither Fronty on the racer's bench nor the old men at Grogan's against the wall, and so his hand asserted itself along her leg. It moved toward the thigh, full and warm with its own heat, until fingers touched the hard elastic. In disbelief he traced this line passionately, while behind him the sky reverberated with fiery displays and the stunning explosions of aerial bombs that echoed off the mountain.

Carefully her hand moved his away—to the thigh.

"Why?" he asked, his mouth thick with excitement.

"Don't."

"Why?" His hand moved upward to the sheer cloth and the tight, flat stomach. Her hand circled his wrist and with a strength that surprised him she placed his hand on his own crotch.

"No dice," she said. "It's the wrong time." As she got up, sweeping her skirt straight, moving toward the car, Mill understood.

"But," he said, on his knees like any member of her gang, "but otherwise you would?"

Her laugh was the sound of exhaust, and when she turned he saw the wide lips, teeth, tip of the tongue. "Man, you're really stupid," she said, hands on her sleek hips. "Why, Gus and the boys would have your nuts. And what do you think *he'd* say if he knew you'd screwed me? Or even tried to?"

"If who knew?" Mill said; his knees trembled with the effort of getting to his feet. "Who do you mean?"

"Why, Tonto, man," she said. "Your little brother."

Chapter 4

As Mill rounded The Curve his lights crossed the darkness, sweeping over the net of cornfield where like a lame animal the twenty-foot convertible waited among the frail, green stalks.

Business for Inner, after hours—

Behind him in the garage was the warm, dark grease of another Friday night. He had borrowed money—from his mother, his sister Audrey, from Fronty—and now the Shelby tubing waited to be cut and bent to conform with the cryptic chalk marks on the garage floor: each kickup and crossmember would articulate the foundation, into which the Offy engine would be dropped. Then the rear end, brakes, suspension—and the other parts which were already rusting to death on the Alpha Romeo coupe in Inner's yard.

And Inner and Fronty—old men both—were not talking now for some thirty years.

He had got the idea for the Sports Special when he took the poster from Hotten's shed. Two mythical racing cars, pipe dreams from the artist's airbrush, hovered off the ground; speed was indicated by lines streaming from tires and the way the rear half of the cars dissolved in color. The words were gold on the blue background: TEN THOUSAND DOLLARS / GRAND PRIX.

The Sports Special would have to be low, light, and streamlined; it would need to have disc brakes, torsion bar suspension, a quick-change rear end, four or five speed transmission—and it would be expensive. Perhaps, he thought, the Sports Special is as much a pipe dream as the cars on the poster, and yet when he began to discuss the idea with Fronty, the builder readily agreed to let him use the Offy engine from a trailered midget race car.

"Listen," Mill had said, "if we coupled the Offy engine to the running gear of a wrecked sports car, wouldn't that be efficient and the least expensive?"

"Ummmm, probably," Fronty had agreed. "Utilizing proper modifications."

"Well, you've got the engine from your midget—with an extra engine for a spare. And Inner's got a wrecked Alpha coupe—"

"Nosir!" Fronty was silent as the coffee went cold. He wanted the Sports Special to be built, to please Mill, but he still harbored the thirty year grudge. It was a pretty noble plan, he said, but with Inner, well, no.

"Ten thousand—"

That was the place to begin, Mill thought, for Fronty had said as much: *Could you make money racing? Some have.* Eventually a dealer would notice the Sports Special and no doubt ask Mill to drive a sponsored car. Then anything could happen: prize money plus a salary, endorsements for shaving cream, carbonated beverages, spark plugs. Country club racing, for sport and money: the U.S. circuit, Sebring, Mexico City, the Bahamas, Europe.

"Well?" he asked.

"I would not," Fronty had said. "With Inner, nosir!"

Again Mill wondered what he was doing in this land of stubborn old men—his only hope was to build the Sports Special and to win the local Grand Prix, and he could not build the car without the necessary parts from the Alpha coupe. But the two old men were not talking at all.

Every night Mill worked long after the others had gone home or toward whatever TV set they parked at, and when the million lights of the city began to blink out he snapped the heavy padlock on the front door of the garage and headed the roadster into the sad, dark night, this time toward the skidding convertible.

Like drivers whose cars now rusted in Inner's wrecking yard, like the driver of the Alpha coupe, the woman had crossed the Galloping Goose tracks and barreled her car into the blind, unmarked Curve. Now it rested in Inner's cornfield, among the broken stubble. Mill's headlights caught the sheen of the woman's gold dress as she lurched across the settled dirt.

"Why in hell don't they have a sign?"

Mill followed his headlight beams across the field. Then he smiled and said, Oh sure, remembering the woman: she had stopped for gas at Fronty's in this same twenty-foot convertible, and had asked whether his roadster was for sale. He remembered too the small dark man who rode with her.

But now she was alone, dressed in gold, impatiently tapping her gold cigarette lighter on the car door. From the lip of The Curve to the car's bumper was a plowed chevron; only the rich black loam had kept the car from rolling over. Under the rear bumper he found the differential bottomed in dirt.

"Well?"

It was his professional opinion they should leave the car for Inner. Long ago he had realized the value of this land and he claimed all rights to whatever car happened to be there in the morning. The corn he planted was not a serious crop, and any ears harvested went, it was said, into mash for the Greeneye.

"Well?"

"Lady, you've got it in here."

"Hell's bells, I know that."

From the highway the roadster's lights cast them in deep shadows, highlighted by the woman's golden sheen. She was tall, and because the dress was tightly belted it emphasized hips which would someday run to sleek, expensive fat.

"Can you?" she asked, and, on his knees by the bumper, he said he would try.

He tried to drive it out, but the wheels churned the soft dirt. Then he eased the roadster onto the field and hooked a tow-cable between the two cars; with this combined power, and an armful of corn stalks under the convertible's rear wheels, the big car rocked toward the pavement. Mill unhooked the cable and stood on the road's edge, laughing. The chevron was wide on entry and narrow on exit, and all the corn between was totaled.

"What's funny?"

She limped to his side, the gold shoes caked with mud and the heel of one torn free; the dress was sparrow-gray along the bottom. Yet, in spite of the mud and the shock of blonde hair that fell like corn-fuzz across her face, she was elegant. Her fist emerged from her purse not with money but a gold cigarette case, which she flicked open to him.

They inhaled deeply in unison, and Mill said: "I was laughing at Inner's face when he sees this tomorrow. I mean it's obvious."

"I always forget about that damn curve." She turned to limp toward her car, then stopped. "Let me buy you a drink. I'm on my way."

He was certain she was, else why had she missed The Curve she knew was there? He hesitated, looked at his blackened coveralls and work boots, and she must have read his mind for she said: "That's okay. I like dirty men."

He left the roadster in the garage and climbed into the deep leather; he heard the emergency brake click out of its slot and felt the smooth acceleration push him down as the dappled twenty-foot convertible roared over the highway, into the abandoned countryside. He knew this road, had tested his roadster on it every morning for years, and now he hugged the door as the woman raced into every curve in tire-shrieking slides. Toes pressed against the floor, he could sense the vibrations of power flowing from engine to driving axles, and he felt unsure without a wheel before him.

When she turned the radio three decibels higher, and pounded on the wheel with her fist, Mill asked: "Where to?"

"It has no name, *reely*. Call it The Place."

Lights caught a rabbit at the road margin. Hypnotized into terror by the brightness, the animal darted out, was chased a few quick feet, and disposed of with a sound like a dropped pumpkin.

Mill knew they were headed toward *nothing:* for thirty miles in this direction there was nothing except a few struggling farms and a general store that long ago had gone out of business. He thought, What the hell, and leaned into the rich leather. There were worse ways to die. Perhaps this was his place—beside the blonde, in the luxury of a deep-sprung swift car, living out of expense accounts and credit cards—perhaps he had been with the old men too long.

There was a second of comfort—the sweet summer breeze, the bright spattering of stars perfectly aligned over the narrow road—before tires squealed hard and the car turned into the bushes. Mill braced his feet as the sky spun in a tight right angle; the trees blurred into the windshield and parted, the car bounced over dirt and rolled smoothly up the tunnel of a wide, tree-lined road. Beyond the twin cement pillars with their ornamental steel arch, the ride ended sharply in a parking lot where bumpers blazed against headlights.

The woman was swimming through darkness for the building, while Mill sat stunned. Over the years he had passed here a thousand times, trees and brush secretary to what he supposed was land not even good enough for logging or pasture. Neither light nor sound came from the dark building but the secret parking lot was filled with expensive cars.

"Come on, boy." Her grip on his arm was solid, pulling him toward the hollow dark of the stairs. Beyond Mill heard muffled·music and voices. As the brass door knocker shattered the night, a postage stamp panel slid aside.

Well well, a voice said. Miss Maloney, well well.

The door swung open, and beside the door, smiling at the woman, glaring at Mill, was a huge man fitted into a tuxedo.

"Used to be a *real* roadhouse in the 'Twenties, rotgut and rods," the woman said, leading Mill down the carpeted stairs, "now it's legit. But boringly select."

People and furniture spun from the red velvet walls, and in the gay blast of laughter Mill suddenly felt absurd. His free hand straightened the greased collar and cuffs and he slid into the room, a man of fashion. But in the great grinning disc of the crowd only a few eyes turned to observe the tall, dirty boy and the taller, mud-spattered, gold-spangled woman. He was a novelty, he thought, like the man and woman in bathing suits at the bar, or the Negro musician who trailed two-hundred feet of extension cord from his electric guitar as he crooned and trilled among the tables.

Mill glanced at the door, as if to prepare his exit, and saw there were now two gorillas; they pointed at Mill for the benefit of a third man, who was shorter and seemed to belong in a suit.

Mill was led to a wheel-sized table; the woman removed her shoes and placed them on the table, where they shed flakes of dried mud.

"Good evening, Miss Maloney." The waiter wore red livery and carried a towel on his arm. "Vat 69, waterback, if I remember correctly?"

"You do. And give these to the cook to clean." She placed the shoes on his drink tray, and reached into her purse to add the missing heel. "Try and tack this on."

The waiter had already turned to leave when Mill said he would have the same; the man nodded and disappeared into the elegant confusion. The woman was reaching into her purse for lipstick when the Negro sidled up chording electronic vibrations. He was followed by a small colored boy who guided the two-hundred feet of extension cord through the room.

The thingsss I wasss yearnin for, wassss piled up on your dresser drawer... Issss majjick

Miss Maloney leaned back in laughter, and her broad shoulders shook with genuine mirth as the Negro leaned closer to flash his eyes and diamond teeth. "Leave thisss dirty boy, Misss Maloney, and I'll see you after the show."

The Negro struck a flat, laughed, and floated into the crowd, followed by the boy in red livery who played out the extension cord, and Mill felt he had already made an enemy.

Two men in wash and wear suits paused to stare at Miss Maloney; they nudged elbows and winked. Together they pulled their jackets straight and started ahead, eyes on her low-cut dress, when the first man tripped over the electric guitar cord.

"Hey, pickaninny!"

"The very left one," said his partner.

When Mill looked at the woman to see if she had heard, her eyes were on him, her face suddenly frozen and serious; the lipstick tube had not finished its swipe and it hung near her chin, the lower lip colorless, drained of blood. Her eyes were points of carbon steel drilling into his, probing behind the retina into gray viscera, into whatever hidden erotic fantasy.

"What's wrong?"

"Nothing," she said, fingers lifting the bright tube to her mouth. "Not. A. Thing. It's just that for a second you looked like someone else. Someone I knew."

Drinks came, double shots, and before Mill could ask who it was he could possibly resemble a man with a clipped mustache and accent dropped into the empty chair. He wore high black riding boots, jodhpurs, and a coat that needed a shave.

"Joan," he said, raising the woman's hand to his lips, "I 'ave ze part for you. You simply must listen."

Mill was startled by the woman's racing laughter; her head was thrown back, laughing, as the man rubbed his mustache into place.

"Honest to gawd, Alfon," she screamed. "Go get us two more. After that line we need them." The man rose to filter into the crowd; Miss Maloney drank off half her whiskey neat and stared into the amber eye of the glass. "That character Alfon. He wants me to be in his stupid movie. He insists I'm another Veronica Lake."

"Why don't you do it?"

41

"Do what?" she asked, eyes narrowing. "Be in his movie? Well his problem is money, and while I don't mind shelling out a little for Culture I'm sure not going to Elay to make an ass of myself—then project the evidence on every screen in the U.S. of A."

The waiter flashed up with two more double shots, waterback, compliments of the Frenchman."

"Frenchman my mother's wazzoo!" she screamed, her mouth bubbling with laughter.

At the bar the man in the swimming suit raised his glass and announced in lush tones: "When in doubt, drink and shout—"

"I never even knew this Place was here," Mill said. "Do you come here often?"

"Everybody's got to find his own Place; I come here when I feel like a fast drive and a fast drink. Gawd knows there's little to do in this town. I can take the Place for about an hour." She smiled and tipped her glass, a fragrant flower.

The second drink brought a network of vines over Mill's head and he gazed into the roaring room where glasses flashed in the muted light—he felt good being with people again, away from the isolated garage with its sweat, grease, and old men. Across from him the woman was silent, moodily staring into her glass, and he wondered: if she was willing to contribute money to a whacky movie, mightn't she consider a sound investment like the Sports Special?

Before he could ask, a man took the empty chair between them. He was squat and balding, the piston dome head polished to an aluminum buff.

"Joanie, how nice." His lips pulled down at the ends when he spoke, and inflated between lines when he cleared his throat. "And your escort?"

The woman laughed and introduced the man as Amphora, the Owner. He ignored Mill's outstretched hand to lean across the table, his teeth clenched: "Where you are without a gun."

"I call him 'Snail' because he's so slimy," Joanie screamed, her finger close to the man's nose, as if she were a collector about to impale a rare red butterfly.

"But kid," Amphora said, slowly shaking his loose jowls, "don't you try it."

From nowhere came another double-shot, which went down with the faint acrid taste of lighter fluid. Mill thought Amphora as good a name as any, and hadn't even considered calling the blunt slug-like man 'Snail.'

"Fantastic place you have here, Mr. Amphora."

Amphora stood up, seemingly without rising from the chair. "I'll see you later, Joanie. And you, too, kid."

Joanie's laughter was mildly hysterical. "It's Mr. Varthis, Amphora Varthis. He's gawdawful sensitive about it. Something about being an immigrant."

"Oh," Mill said, sensing he'd made another enemy.

"Well, he's done all right in this country." Mill was reminded of his loose, dirty coveralls as he watched the baggy pants of Amphora climb the stairs; the heads of the two gorillas bent close to the aluminum piston dome, to listen.

Alfon filtered back, heels clicking beside the table like ice cubes. "Ze contract," he said, holding Joanie's hand between his, sliding finely manicured fingers over hers in an oil and water movement.

"Son," Joanie laughed, "let me tell you about Alfon. He *reely* was in Hollywood, at the studios, and he had a very lucrative racket going: he sold the lingerie of the stars to his deviant friends. Isn't that a scream? Can't you see one of his portly transvestites bridled into Marilyn Monroe's brassiere and Grace Kelly's panties? The dirtier the garment the more he could ask. Isn't that a riot?

Alfon inspected his cuticles, faintly smiling at this recall of the old days, and Mill, amazement undiminished, asked if that was true.

"Of course, dear boy. Why not? It was a legitimate enterprise, and profitable. *Par exemple,* once a nightgown from a very famous actress, best unnamed here, went for fifteen hundred. Not what one might call penny-ante."

"Fifteen hundred DOLLARS?" Joanie screamed. She leaned forward, serious lines chiseled on her face. "Tell me, Alfon. Were they very dirty?"

"Don't be crude, my dear."

Suddenly Mill felt a need for relief. Alfon pointed out the men's room and even offered to escort him. Mill declined, rose unsteadily into the lurching dancers, and once in motion his feet accelerated to the music; in the paneled mirrors along the dance floor he saw his white and black coveralls topped with a sheepish grin. The room revolved with dancers and the spectrum of colored lights, and he reeled into a table; snatched back, he was shuffled like a card into the line. His work-hard hands fell on the warm, bare midriff before him, and two hands clamped on his waist from behind, to lock him in the keyway of dancers.

Do the bunny, do the bunny—

The line pranced sideways, Mill's feet flopping in giggling steps, his hands sliding down the smooth, absolute contours of the woman's butt, and the line jerked forward.

—hop   hop   hop

Mill's eyes followed the fleshy contours of the woman's backbone upward, past the halter, to the pearl necklace. He thought how a simple flick with his teeth would open the clasp.

"Got any phony idears?" The grip on his shoulder was heavy; he sighted along the hairy back-hand and foreshortened arm to see the small bright eyes of the gorilla.

The line raced ahead, snatching Mill off, until the hand landed again and jerked him from the file. "Any phony idears?"

"Phony ideas?"

"False I.D.," Amphora said, stepping from behind a potted plant. "To prove you're twenty-five."

As the second gorilla grabbed his arm, Mill said: "What is this? I thought it was twenty-one."

"It's twenty-five in my place," Amphora said. "Toss him out. He's a bum, and underage."

"Wait," Mill said, thinking of Joanie, her money, and the unfinished drink he had left; pulling one arm loose from the encircling hands he fumbled in his deep coverall pocket for the billfold. "Here, see I'm ok."

Amphora took the ragged piece of leather and sorted through a stack of shabby cards, check stubs, and useless receipts. "Millard Sederstrom," he said, memorizing the name on the driver's license. Then Mill saw the blazing ring on Amphora's finger, and he remembered the passenger in the twenty-foot convertible that day it had stopped at Fronty's for gas—Amphora, small and dark and evil behind the windshield.

He handed the mess back to Mill. "Get out, kid, and leave Joanie alone. If you bother her again, I'll personally burn you."

"Okay, sure," Mill agreed, backing away until the three men were far down a distant tunnel. He didn't want to leave Joanie, the only source of wealth he knew, but neither did he want to get burned. But the hand that next gripped his coveralls was Joanie's, naked and white. The pins were out of her hair and it tumbled loosely into her inclined breasts.

She had ordered Fallout Flasks, and her grip wrestled him into the chair, held him before the fizzling glasses. From the corner of his eye he saw Amphora and the gorillas, heads together.

"Well. And did you invest in the movie?"

"Alfon finagled a tentative promise—not that I expect a return on my investment."

The Sports Special, he knew, would exist forever as dreams and a pile of Shelby tubing unless he got some funds, and he could not count on Inner and Fronty to be united any more than he could expect his father to win a quiz show or Tonto to get a scholarship to Harvard. "Do you," he said, leaning toward her—he saw the three men crossing the room and at the same instant felt the tic clawing at his cheek, tugging the mouth into a fictitious smile of terror—and he had only seconds to say: "Do you invest often—in projects like that?"

"You dear boy," she said, her hands coming together as if in prayer and moving against his face, clasping the stubble streaked cheeks, probing the dirt. "Such innocence."

Cool fingers came from the smoky mist and he went limp, as if something important inside had snapped like a rubber band. He saw the sweet face tilted against the swaying room, skin bronze, hair and gown gold; the exhaust of perfume swelled from a cavity somewhere and he saw himself drunk in the forest of rich golden hair, riding the white convertible to the rich fields of her earth.

Ohhhhh how we dansssed on the night we wusssss wed, danssed and we danssed till we fell out of bed

The tic raced across his body to claw at his groin and leave his legs trembling—in frustration, or in anger at the guitar player and his insipid cord guide, or simply in need of relief. Her arms fell away and he lurched into the crowd again, bladder screaming, to cross the dance floor in a mambo rock, colored lights rotating in his eyes. In the paneled mirrors he saw his reflection and swore that next time he'd have a tie and white shirt and credit cards, all stolen if necessary, and he would compete on his own terms: he *did* belong in this crazy din, drinking good whiskey, eating lobster, and turning the wheel of the twenty-foot convertible. He pushed through the dancers, who had shifted to a riot Charleston marathon, and did a soft-shoe exit down the narrow hallway.

"When in doubt," the bather declared, far away, "drink and shout."

The hallway was eternal.

Two pinkish lights like nostrils, miles apart, glistened overhead. His bladder had expanded to breaking when he reached the first door, marked Private. Beside it stood Amphora, soft pink light flowing around his shoes.

"Straight ahead, sonny."

Mill stumbled toward the distant light, fingers trailing along each wall for guidance. He was almost to the second light when he felt hands cup his armpits and the hall's end rushed toward him in the blackness of thirty-weight oil. His feet kicked back hard into empty air; the door opened, he was lifted and, with a fluid motion, thrown into the night. His feet missed the pleated steps and he landed on asphalt, rolling like a hoop into the bumper of a new Lincoln.

Immobile, he closed his eyes against the glare of chrome and far away he heard hands clapping, as if being dusted after dirty work.

"That's just a sample, sonny." The door slammed, punctuating the night.

Mill rolled into the darkness between two cars, wondering what it meant to be "burned"—and he knew with a sudden clarity that this Place was not his, that a credit card and tuxedo would open no doors for him, that he belonged in Grogan's where men in hard hats drank soapy beer under the yellow gaze of the ragged deer heads, and listened to Detroit cowboys on the jukebox sing of lost loves, lost buddies, lost chances.

Knowing this, his hand reached out to touch the shiny, cold sun of a hubcap. He rolled to his left side and, his face reflected vague and formless in the dark, the screwdriver from his pocket was slid under the valve stem.

There was a *pop,* like expensive champagne opened, and the air bubbled out. The heavy Lincoln nosed down as Mill scooted to the rear and when the second valve stem was out the car tilted and settled, hip-high.

Mill rolled to the next car, the screwdriver tip slipping into the soft rubber of the valve stem, and as that machine began to heel over he was already crawling behind the endless bright bumper softly laughing, his pain forgotten.

When he finally slipped through the brush the moon shone on angled roofs, and the parking lot resembled Inner's wrecking yard, where cars hunched together like lovers in the final embrace of death.

Only Joanie's car stood upright, on rich, full tires.

Mill parted the trees and began to run down the road over shards of moonlight, laughing, coveralls slapping his legs. A repair man would be needed tomorrow and the nearest garage was Fronty's—he tried to see the evening in the only terms he knew: a ledger, listing profits and loss.

Chapter 5

"Now," the company man said, "because gas sales are higher than in thirteen years—"

Mill thought: Fronty will not fix up this place. Fronty wishes to sit out his days in this tin can patched building that heels over like a racer in a tight turn—the unpaved lot, the unsafe lube pit, the foggy windows through which he can see the vanished past. Further, he will not because the man in the blue wash and wear suit is a company slicker. Last, he will not because he is stubborn.

Which, Mill well knew, was why Fronty would not round The Curve to Inner's yard to look at the Alpha Romeo coupe, because they were two stubborn old men who had not spoken to each other for more years than Mill had lived.

The slicker gestured, smiled, bit his lower lip, and assumed a question mark stance, hands slack on hips—as if to say that he, the company sales representative, a babe in arms, had sure fallen into a pit of hard dealers and, yes sir, they were putting something over. Then his expression changed to dismay.

Why, Mill thought, it's disintegrating.

Across the parking the slicker stomped in angry steps. He stopped at the rear fender of his red, white, and blue car and looked back, to see if the cripple had changed his mind; then gravel spit from the tires and as the rocks still rained down the car was already around The Curve and across the rusty Galloping Goose tracks.

"Company field representative," Fronty said, running his palms over the wheels at each side. "Wanted to paint the place company colors. Y'hear? He wanted to paint this damn place red, white, and blue, like a flag. Because sales're higher than in thirteen years."

But Fronty would not. Mostly, because he was stubborn.

Snuff pulled on his pipe, the exhaust of a slow idle, and reviewed the past in the speedway of his mind, where there was a pileup at every curve. Fronty parked his chair and surveyed with satisfaction his trashland estate. Mill shifted off the Coke machine and into low as wheels rattled across the gravel. The company sales representative returning, he thought, but the threatening roar of dual exhausts drove a scoop-shovel, raked Mercury sedan across the parking.

The Mercury rocked at the island, the driver's head cocked forward; the engine revved through gutted mufflers.

More junk, Mill thought, as he waited beside the gas pumps, the heat and dust swirling from under the car. When the engine switched off he was aware of the tense silence; the field insects had stopped buzzing, leaving only the distant angry stutter of the chain saw high on the mountain.

The driver swung off the seat to face Mill, and Gus, in cycle leathers, came from the other side to prop open the hood.

"A race, man. What say?"

The driver pushed back his cycle cap, sleeked the dust from his sideburns, and kicked at the hot gravel with heavy, stomping boots. While he waited for Mill's answer he unrolled his black tee-shirt sleeve and revealed the pack of cigarettes.

"A flatout, balls-out race to Damascus and back." He carefully placed the cigarette between his teeth and leaned forward. "For a fin?"

"Sheeut." But the single word emerged flat from Mill's tight, dry throat. Under his coveralls he itched; sweat and grime surrounded his pounding heart, which accelerated from fear. A killing heat flashed from the dusty parking, and he leaned against the gas pump to control his knees. "Sheeut. That wouldn't even buy a headlight on my car."

"Then twenty, man. But man we ain't trying to wreck no cars—the idea is to *GO.*"

"Not for a hundred," Mill said, the words dry in his throat. "Now, can I sell you some gas?"

Gus moved past the battered fender but the driver stuck out his hand. "Cool it, Gus. If the cat's worried about his wheels, if he's chicken—"

Mill saw Gus's fist clench and he knew that behind the dark glasses the driver's eyes were hot with anger and he feared the sense of death that spun on the brilliant air.

They turned in military unison toward the Merc. The driver hesitated, hands locked around the door post, the unlit cigarette clenched between his teeth, and said: "If you feel the need, man, ask for Marty. That's me."

The door crashed shut, the engine fired, raising clouds of fine dust from under the gutted mufflers, shaking the empty countryside with the sound of gunfire. "See you around, man." Wheels spun, churning a machine-gun spray of gravel over the station; tires shrieked at the road and the car was gone in a cloud of blue oil smoke, gutted mufflers, and the small cold suns of flashing hubcaps.

It was a No Sale.

"Gawddammit, Fronty," Mill said, turning angrily through the swirling dust. "We could at least oil that gravel"

With a sudden anger he lit a cigarette and picked up a wrench, which he sent flying through the lube room to crash against the work bench. Following its flashing arc he saw the crater of the lube pit, that concrete walk-down bomb shelter, and beyond the smear of dark floor the rhythm of wrenches, box and open end, crescent and spanner, stillson and ratchet, aligned by type and length on the wallboard. Below the work bench stood the bare rudiments of the Sports Special: a trapezoid of three sizes Shelby tubing.

Mill opened a warm Coke and hoisted himself on the battered pop machine, his legs swinging. He needed the parts from the wrecked Alpha Romeo, and he tried to dream up reasons why the old men should be friends again.

"The Sports Special will be a good investment. For publicity."

"Publicity," Fronty drawled, "I don't need. Nor trading stamps. Service and quality sell gas."

People stopped to spend their money at Fronty's, and the roadster was an advertisement. Because gas sales were now higher than in thirteen years.

But Fronty was stubborn.

"The prize money in the Grand Prix," Mill said.

"The Gran Pree money we'll get."

In his wheelchair a thin man with thin sandy hair and negligible eyebrows, which gave his face a total lack of expression—although one might consider his fading freckles, slowly being replaced by liver spots, as expressive—he didn't need those parts, or advertising, or trading stamps just as he didn't need the use of his legs.

"Not without those Alpha Romeo parts," Mill said.

"We'll build the torsion bar suspension. Use the midget's steering. Make other parts."

Mill saw his dream melting in the hot fire of the old feud.

"But the Alpha has everything we need. The Sports Special will cost us almost nothing."

"Nosir! Mill Sederstrom," Fronty said, his voice fading. "I would not go down there—have not been to that yard for thirty years."

"Sure, we don't need the Alpha coupe. We can get expensive parts."

Except they had no money.

Again Mill wondered what he was doing in this land of stubborn old men—penniless, hopeless, learning no trade except the art of survival. To return to this edge of the city service station, with no future here except sweat, grease, and busted knuckles; unable to earn enough money to get out of town; unwilling to look for another job, and unfit for other work if he should find it.

The single hope, glowing and diminishing in dreams, was the Sports Special and the ten thousand dollars.

Again he thought of Joanie, and wondered whether she would be willing to lend him the money. He had tried to telephone but her number was not in the directory; he had called Information but the operator said that number could not be given out. He had driven his morning speed run very slowly this week, an eye out for the shadowy mansion, the parking lot, the twin cement pillars. But he couldn't find The Place; it was as if the brush had grown up to screen the roadhouse from his sight.

Now in frustrated anger he dropped the empty pop bottle into its square and crossed the dirt-packed yard, to climb into the burning leather of his roadster. He jabbed the starter button and heard the engine catch; the throb steadied with a kick on the throttle. He cruised through the station, fighting a desperate impulse to plant his right foot to the floor, to pop the clutch, and knock the flimsy building down with his exhaust, to bury the debris under gravel from his wheels. But he refrained from pity and when Fronty asked where he was going, Mill shouted: "To talk Inner into coming *here.*"

Fronty was shouting, "He won't. *He's* stubborn," and Mill was on the street, the roadster's grill lunging toward The Curve. He ached to kick the gas feed, to scream past Inner's yard, past home and family, past Hubert's (Open All Nite) Drive-Inn and Eddie, out of the city and away, blocked on all sides by stubborn old men.

Exhaust muffled, he cruised the short, easy three-quarters of a country mile.

Facing The Curve, and this side of the rusting trolley tracks, was the board fence, itself a wreck, with the thousand suns of hubcaps and the faded letters: INNER MCMAHON, Prop.

He was reflected in the rusty mirrors of hubcaps as he swung the axle against the suspended driveline. The sounds of industry rang across the battered, humped tops and sightless windshields: the end of a long line from Detroit. Metallic sound still lapped the ruined bodies as Inner came from the small room behind the office, struggling with his fly. The grizzled cheeks, troll lips moved, the grease-stained eyebrows arced in recognition–then the smile quickly dissolved, for he anticipated Mill's purpose.

"The crip with you?" he asked, his head leaning in the direction of the world beyond the fence.

Mill said no and the junky motioned him into the black cave, to the security of the A-Grade cowhide backseat; the Greeneye was out beside two piston cups.

"Up yours, m 'boy," Inner said, drinking, wiping the skidmark of stubble on his chin, digging into his bib pocket for a cigarette. "Up yours." As he reached to hold the tire at his middle, anticipating the explosive warmth of the liquor, he said: "Figgered a way to get the hell out of this bizness. Ennyway this phase of it. Antique Restorations, Incorporated, I'm calling it. Why there's lots of folks' hobby is restoring old cars. Nice people, too: doctors, lawyers, professional men. No crum-bums. Just fine folks with a hobby."

Mill waited, his eyes on the prettiest of the calendar girls above Inner's desk; as Inner growled and dreamed Mill saw Joanie Maloney's face slide onto the calendar body: idealized, anatomical, provocative–and paper. Or Eddie: her nude sex kitten body teetering on womanhood, the breasts too high, too cupped, nipples too soft as she danced across parking lots pointing out ruined fenders.

"I'm thinking," Inner announced, his fist striking the tin desk with a thunderous rolling sound, "I'm thinking of even putting an *advertisement* in the paper!"

"That's real progressive, Inner."

"I'm using my noodle–I'm not gonna mess up like I did during the war. I could've sold tires, gas coupons, batteries, motors at black-market prices, I could've made a fortune, I–" His eyes rolled toward the roof, a jungle of dark rust, and his mind swirled into the collisions and mistakes of yesteryear: things could have been different, before the board fence began to lean with its own weight.

After he had the old cars cleared out he was thinking of sports cars exclusively. Big money. Very showy. All parts tagged and binned. Also a finer clientele. Cigars and trimmed mustaches.

When he said this Mill realized that Inner knew how badly they wanted the Alpha.

"Yore workin' for him, ain 'tcha?"

"What would you take?" Mill asked. "It would be *cash,* of course." There was no need to anger him, and Inner was a dickering man. Cash talked.

"What's a nice boy like you, with a collich edjucation, want to work in a two-bit place like that for? The years go by–"

Any explanation about school would be lost on Inner, as it would be lost on Mill's family or even Fronty–how could he explain what he didn't understand?–so Mill said: "We won't buy parts. Cheaper to take it off your hands total, to the satisfaction of all."

"–and you don't know where time went. Yore young, got plans, worlds of time–"

Inner poured himself another shot; he bumped along the rough road of life, drifted into a sweeter world.

"–and then wake up on a damn black Monday and the world and you are old–"

"Cash on the barrel-head. Take it off your hands."

"–and and, oh if'n I had it to do again, I'd I'd–"

Make the same mistakes, Mill thought. Careen into this scrap-pile world where time stops, wallow in an eternity of junkyards, wrecks without end: stasis versus speed, wreckers versus racers. It'd be no different.

Which caused Mill to ask: "Mr. McMahon, what *did* happen between you and Fronty? That you don't talk?"

"Cash is it?" he roared. Then gently he turned in a broadsliding four wheel drift to lay his peened hand on Mill's knee. "One condition. You come to work for me. You know about cars, got an edjucation, class. We'll get us a finer bunch of customers. Get rid of all this junk. Build the joint up. Everything racked and binned, tagged. Square the yard away." He rose and went to the door, lulled by this absurd fantasy of rejuvenation.

"Paint the fence?"

"Replace it," Inner said, "with one to stand cyclones. Let the people see our merchandise when we ain't here, weekends off. Also paid vacations, hospital plan, fringe benefits."

"Maybe landscape the yard," Mill said, goading the old man. "Murals on the office. Junk sculpture near the entrance." Faced on one side by Fronty, the builder, who would not make a single improvement; on the other by Inner, the destroyer, the wrecker, who built a junkyard of dreams: Mill could not win.

He got up and walked through the doorway, suppressing the same anger he had felt at Fronty's. He walked quickly past the driveshaft gate posts, the perimeter of hoops of tire halves, the tilted board fence. Over the noise of roaring exhaust, of skimming, squealing tires, of crashing gravel, he heard the crazed, frantic bark: "If'n he wants it, he's got to come here! "

Mill's foot on the floor in fury, the rear tires protesting as the gearshift lever rams into second at five thousand rpms, and after clearing Inner's cornfield trap the road is a long black tape, the station a blur as Mill shifts into high, the blur of Fronty raising from the wheelchair and Snuff staggering off the bench eyes cupped against the sun.

The roadster races toward the narrowing point of road, where all lines converge. The car rocks between the expansion strips until it is sailing over their tips, the tires barely touching the asphalt. Wind rushes at Mill's eyes, bringing real tears.

The speedometer needle hangs at ninety.

As the first curve approaches the forest folds in like a dead-end.

Mill keeps his foot on the gas through the gentle angle and prepares for the bad S-curve by shifting up a cog to catch the bend in a power slide. Tires skim the pavement and barely hang to the road rim; he measures the margin of safety by the swirls of dust, the dervish ripples that indicate the right rear tire is two inches of rubber into danger.

Exhaust and engine sing, the country air shatters before the car like glass, and the gauges dance in their circles.

He speeds across the sky, down a rainbow, to the inevitable pot of gold of which he dreams. For in the freedom of flight, of fantasy, he is not the pawn of two old men, nor the family buffer, nor his brother's keeper, but:

Mill Sederstrom, blazing the last lap toward the ten thousand dollars, the champagne-filled trophy cup, the Hollywood starlet who will pucker hot, moist lips. He will stand on the car seat smiling for the klieg lights of flashbulbs: the boy champion. The Ford transmission is a six speed gearbox, the flathead V-8 a dual overhead cam, all aluminum, highly tuned balls out racing engine designed to the last cotter key by Carrera Sederstrom, Inc.

A curve approaches–down a gear, then another, with the dual explosions, the engine wound tight. The car slides again to the breaking point in a perfect four wheel drift–the rim of the road, the world, over to the rim of the universe–and at the final, ultimate moment the foot plants the pedal to the floor and the roadster regains equilibrium, pulls through the curve into the undemanding straight, Victory Lane, with fields clipping past like the ripple of laid paper.

Also he is Dick Seaman, lone Englishman on the pre-war Mercedes team: suave, cool, international, fast.

Same curve, same instant: Phil Hill in a Ferrari, golden boy, California, sunshine, up through the ranks to fortune.

Especially he is the greatest of them all: Tazio Nuvolari, pounding on the door panel for more speed, coughing blood through the white surgical mask drawn tightly over the gaunt, expiring face; racing with a vengeance against death which only speed can satiate.

The tach needle eclipses the red line and he keeps the pedal to the floor until the engine peaks its screaming optimum and then he eases his foot back, to let flight pass the car. To slow for the gentle return run to the garage saturated in sweet grease; to view again the unfinished chassis and the mirage of ten thousand dollars he is certain he can win. Back to sweaty coveralls, dust drifting down his neck, more debts and the old, old men.

Back for the five o'clock rush hour.

Chapter 6

When Saturday was a rosy haze falling between houses and towering fir trees, softening everything, Mill nosed his father's Edsel toward town. He whistled softly between his teeth, smelling his own sweet breath: he had bathed away the dust which fell on him from fender wells, shaved twice, and now he felt clean in every pore. He had put on a jacket, tie, and a white shirt and as he walked from the house, the keys to the Edsel jingling in his hand, he could feel the pride his parents felt at seeing their son dressed up. *Have fun, have fun,* his mother said, and suddenly he knew he had been isolated in the garage for too long. Too many nights he had stayed with the old men, or worse, had stayed alone. Tonight, he vowed, things would be different.

The Edsel's floor was ankle-deep in dirt, and the sun-faded Indian blanket on the seat held the sweet odor of cigar smoke, but the car moved away from the curb with a sluggish respectability. Mill glanced in the rear-view mirror, and saw an orchid colored coupe nose through the ball game at the corner. Twice he had seen the same car parked on this street, and now he viewed it carefully. Uneasy thoughts cruised his mind about Marty, Gus, and that gang, as the orchid coupe diminished in the mirror; he turned the comer, but was not followed, and when he had circled the block the car was gone.

The wheel, large and unnatural in his hands, steered the Edsel past the boys' ballgame and slowly out of the neighborhood. Foster Road was almost empty, Loaner's Comer was a sleepy intersection where only the taverns showed their neon. He wanted to get away from all this, to get into the life of the downtown area where people were happy. He was thinking of going to a good restaurant, perhaps a place where he could order from a menu in French, but where Foster and Powell streets intersected he saw the Pink Pail. Because he could remember when it had been called the Cressy Tavern–a room like Grogan's, of dark wood and snappy signs–he recognized this as the ultimate change, but he pulled the Edsel into the parking lot because he thought he might meet someone that he used to know, even after all these years.

The changes were immediately obvious. Windows were boarded shut, and from the doorway, where a man in a derby was checking J.D., an electronic honky-tonk piano spread hysteria. Over the tinny notes, louder by decibels, he heard laughter.

"See some idee, citizen?"

Like a vision from The Place, the man in the derby kept his hand on Mill's arm. As he reached for his billfold Mill noticed the man's red and white striped barbershop quartet shirt, and the purple garter around his upper sleeve. Then he recognized the face, although it had aged greatly in seven years, falling to pouches and a network of fine wrinkles. They had been in high school together: Ron Something, a football player, a club joiner, one of the boomer-boys who stood in the main hall between classes. But Mill's name on the driver's license didn't register, for he said: "So's your grandma. And watch out for the automation. Over-mechanization."

Mill walked into the windowless dark, where all surfaces were painted charcoal black. He felt for the empty stool at the bar's end, and heard a voice asking, "Beer?" Mill nodded, and laid fifty cents on the bar. "One more."

"No, I'll drink this one first."

"I mean another four-bits, buddy."

He paid, thinking that the glass was only slightly larger than those at Grogan's, but cost three times as much. The mug had been iced and silver beads crusted its sides. Perhaps it came from Bavaria, he thought, grinning at the travel posters on the walls: idealistic castles high over the Rhine, an announcement that Manolete would fight a bull in Barcelona on a certain Sunday, and Japan beckoned.

Laughter tinkled like ice, and he turned to see three tanned blondes wearing UO sweatshirts; between each girl sat a tanned, shining boy. White, laughing teeth turned toward the dim light. Before Mill was able to see if he could recognize any of them, a shadow passed across his eyes and he felt his hand being pumped.

"Millard Sederstrom! For crying out loud. It's been years."

A strange face surfaced: crew-cut, horn-rimmed glasses, a silly grin above the long polished jaw, and as his hand was released Mill saw a distant picture from the school year-book. He remembered the face only because during one term of high school he and this boy had been together for every class—it was an association based on a fluke of scheduling.

"Ahh, you've forgotten. It's Karl, Karl Mueller. I knew you right away. You haven't changed a bit. Say, can I buy you a beer?"

Mill nodded and said, "You too." Karl slid his beer and change along the bar, and got on the stool beside Mill.

"Hay Ron! Comin' atcha!"

From the darkness a figure slid past—a balding man, a white apron flapping over his suit, his hands clutching at air, feet sliding smoothly as if on roller skates. Mill rotated to see Ron Something catch the man by the collar and deliver him a hard kick in the seat. Without hesitation the man flew out the door and into the night. The room burst with laughter.

"That's Donnie, the Sliding Waiter," Karl said, wiping his eyes and laughing. "He works at a bar downtown and comes in here half-gowed. Every Saturday he gets the boot—it's a tradition."

Mill turned to his beer and Karl was saying, "It's really good to see you. It takes me back quite a few years. I guess that's why I returned, because things don't seem to change. I like this town, and I'd like my kids to grow up here."

You haven't changed a bit. Karl's phrase stirred waves of surprise—he had thought the past seven years had changed him a great deal. After the army and five years of college, he knew he was not whatever he had been. Mill was amazed that Karl saw no change in this city where he saw everywhere the alteration of growth, the steady insistent destruction of the past but he only coughed and said: "How many do you have?"

"Well, none yet;" Karl said, again looking into his beer, almost blushing. "In fact, I'm not even married—but I will be soon, I hope. How about you?"

"Me? No, I'm not married."

"There's plenty of time."

"Yes." Mill's cheek jerked, a strong undertow near the bone. No change, he said, and plenty of time—but there wasn't. Time was a great wheel, accelerating faster and faster to an optimum until centrifugal force would take over and the wheel, coasting, would slow to a stop.

"Say, weren't you back east at school, someone was saying—"

"Yeah, architecture. I just got home."

"That's great! I got my B.S. at State, in electrical engineering; did a year of research in England, and then worked for Aerospace, until the smog and the freeways got to be too much, and now I've got a good job at Textronics. I intend to live in this city the rest of my life, get married, have some kids, and mow the lawn." He blinked and quickly looked down, as if this were a curious admission.

Mill drank his beer, uneasy with this conversation. He suddenly realized that Karl was the first person his own age he'd met in the month that he'd been back home, and he waited nervously for the next question: *Where are you working?* He knew he could never explain his job at Fronty's: *Well you see I kinda wanted to keep things simple and so I—*

Karl leaned his face toward Mill's ear and pointed to the side room. "You know, it's ironic how things turned out. I mean, *we* weren't anything in high school, you and I—if you don't mind me saying so—we were sure never elected Joe

Freshman or anything. But look in there. You recognize those guys?"

Mill turned his head slightly and through the open doorway he saw four men at a table. Even with the poor light, and the passage of years, he recognized them as boys from his high school class. Again the names escaped him—except for one, Kenny Sooner, an aptly named athlete and lover. Like Ron at the door, they had grown heavy as football muscles eased into fat; not only at the belt-line, but their jaws, cheeks, the flesh over their eyes bulged. If he and Karl had not changed, the four at the table had grown from boys to men, and their heaviness gave them the air of serious maturity. In their well-cut summer suits they looked like executives planning a high level merger of four corporations.

"Remember those guys?" Karl asked. "The big guns in high school, voted most popular, most likely to succeed. Every Monday we'd read in the school paper which girls they'd taken to the postgame dance, and how many touchdowns they'd scored. Know what they're doing now?" As Mill shook his head Karl's voice changed from mild rage to vindictive triumph. "Salesmen, laborers—one sells gyppo used cars down the street, another sells shoes; that guy works in his dad's gas station, and the fourth drives a garbage truck. To look at them you'd think the bastards were bank presidents or something. And you can generalize from this: the people who were really something in high school turned out to be *bums!*" He laughed sharply, and removed his glasses to rub his eyes. "High school was all a joke—yet it seemed so damn serious."

Mill watched the four at the table in mild confusion. He could sympathize with Karl, but he could also identify with the four who had managed—consciously or unconsciously to keep their lives simple. Unlike Karl, he didn't feel any antagonism toward them, then or now; he had been vaguely aware that they existed, but high school had been a series of days he endured, sitting in classes with his jacket on, as if ready at any minute to go home and work on his car.

The ice had melted from glasses, to water the warm mouthful of beer that lay in each, and Mill put a five on the bar. "Get two more, I'll be right back." He slid off the stool and went through the open doorway, past the table, and followed the arrows to the Men's. It was a small green room, smelling of urine, and as he stood at the toilet bowl he read the wall scribblings: *My Mother Made Me a Homo* someone had written, and below it, scratched in the paint, was a reply: *If I Give Her the Wool will She make me one too?* There was a primitive drawing of a man and woman with oversize genitalia, and a phone number. A small sign announced that *Doretta K eats cock* 351-5827. There had been a girl in high school named Doretta Kong—a heavy girl, with huge breasts, who had a reputation as an easy lay; one night, it was rumored, she had gone down for all the members of a social club in exchange for their pins. Mill hadn't known whether to believe any of this, but in his sexual dreams it was always she who walked nude with him across The Point. He had never spoken to her—afraid of what people would say—but now, as if to challenge the assertions of rumor, he wrote the phone number on the back of a match book. Doretta K., of course, might not even be the girl he was thinking of, but it could still be interesting—as long as things were kept simple.

He emerged into the laughter from the bar side, and he was thinking of the blonde's tanned, upturned face, the row of even, sparkling teeth that sent laughter soaring over the roar of electronic music—thinking how great it would be to screw her on a dreamy, euphoric bed—when he felt a hand grab his wrist. The Pink Pail was getting crowded, drinkers sat on the billiards table and the shuffleboard machine, others stood along the walls, and in the dense crowd he couldn't see whose arm held his.

"Hay! Don't I know you?"

Kenny Sooner still wore his hair short, a crew-cut which bristled from the scrubbed scalp; he would go from the locker room to baldness without difficulty. Below the light fringe of hair was the heavy, hard face of an athlete or drill sergeant, and it was impossible to tell if his grimace was a smile.

"I believe so. I'm Mill Sederstrom. We went to school together. "

"He believes so, for crissakes. Hell yes, we know you. We never forget an old school chum, do we, men? Pull up a chair, for crissakes, and sit down." He released Mill's arm and shifted his legs under the table. But there were no empty chairs, and Mill had that beer waiting at the bar. He tried to excuse himself with a wave, but Ken's hand shot out to hold him.

"What're you doing these days?" another man asked.

Mill thought his name was Gary—or Jerry?—and vaguely remembered him as a guy who had gone through a series of pretty sharp cars in a short time. The school paper used to run a notice on the front page every time he got his driver's license back, as a humorous warning to pedestrians.

"Oh, this and that. Looking for a job right now," Mill said. He felt uncomfortable beside the table, as if they were all freshmen again and he was passing by during lunch hour.

"Ever sold cars?"

"No," Mill laughed. "I'm in architecture. I just finished studies at M.I.T."

"Well hay!" Ken said, releasing Mill's arm and taking out a pen. "Let's write that down. We're making plans for the big class reunion, and we want to get all the dope on everybody. Let's see, how do you spell MIT?"

Everyone, including Mill, laughed, and Ken, struggling with his pen, said: "Got that. Now what did you do in high school?"

"You never really did anything in high school, did you?" the third man said. "I mean, anything we could write down. You were just kind of *there.*"

"Yeah, I suppose so," Mill said.

"Still fooling around with cars?" Gary asked, but Mill couldn't tell whether he wanted an answer. The four were coming on like ghosts from his past, and suddenly he remembered how miserable high school had been—how he had avoided classes to stay home and work on his roadster; how self-conscious he had been wearing wide bottom cords and an old flannel shirt, or that blazing silk jockey jacket his mother had bought for him. Again he moved toward the bar, but Ken's hand was quicker.

"Hay, let's see—what girls did you go out with?" "You never did go out with girls, did you?"

"He's as queer as old Karl over there," the fourth man said. Mill thought it strange the two whose names he couldn't remember were the most hostile. He looked from the hand on his wrist to Karl at the bar, and heard the man say: "They are both a couple of un-American queers. They probably Greek each other."

"Now cut it out," Ken said, laughing. "Mill likes girls. Why, I bet he even wrote down Doretta's phone number off the john wall. C'mon, didn't you?"

"Why would he do that? Karl will blow him."

"Naw, Mill's okay," Ken said, releasing his arm to feel the material of his jacket. "Nothing wrong with him that a good suit of clothes won't fix."

"Bullshit!" said the third man, pushing his chair back from the table. "He's a dirty greaseball. I didn't like him then and I don't now."

Mill was baffled, and as amazement shifted to rage he felt the tic claw at his cheek, pulling his mouth into a fictitious smile. As he turned toward the bar the fourth man said:

"Going home to clean Karl's plugs?"

"Fuck you buddy," Mill said, and fear moved him past the doorway to the bar. Beyond the wall he heard the four break into whoops of laughter, and one shouted: "Up your bunny with a meatball. sonny."

At the bar Karl sat with his legs delicately crossed, and his hand held a cigarette in an ivory holder—he is a goddamn fairy, Mill thought, and he drank his warm beer standing up.

"I was wondering," Karl said, "since you just got home, I was wondering if you're interested in a job—I could ask at Textronics—"

"What kind of job? A blow job?" Mill chugged his warm beer and started for the door.

"What did those bastards tell you?" Karl asked, his hand gripping Mill's jacket, pulling him back into the noise. "Surely you can't take them seriously—they're bums, nobodies."

"Go on," Mill said, and as the tic jerked at his cheek he pushed Karl backward, into the bar. He was half-turned toward the door when he felt his arms wrenched together from behind and pushed upward; there was a tearing sound and a terrific pain pierced his shoulders as he was lifted, moved through the doorway. He sailed over the sidewalk in slow motion: the faces of spectators passed his—he saw their eyes open in hot astonishment and then slowly relax to good-humored laughter. One woman, a blonde, pushed back some loose hair and said, "Oh my"; Mill wondered if they had been in high school together, for she looked awfully familiar. Then he was past, and as the street floated toward him, the ribbons of tail-lights streaming like time exposure, his legs touched the sidewalk and the camera shifted to high-speed. His feet were running somewhere behind when he saw the broad expanse of metal rushing at him. Then he tripped, and sprawled heavily against the car's fender; with one foot wedged between the curb and tire he slid sideways into the gutter.

"You want to watch out for automation, citizen. It'll get you every time." Ron Something stood in the doorway, adjusting the derby so it tilted across one watery eye.

Mill unkinked his arms, found that they would support his weight, and got his foot loose. Both sleeves of his jacket were torn at the upper seams—the cuffs hung loosely over his hands, as if designed for a clown's act. He moved quickly toward the Edsel, wild with anger, thinking once again: *To hell with them all—*

He drove with a quiet fury, pushing the car to its limit, past the bleary neon of Loaner's Comer, past the last houses, where families sat before the TV's mild violence, past the city's limits. The Galloping Goose tracks were a ripple under the heavy sedan; gas pedal to the floor, the drive machinery tightened up and the car mushed ahead, into the dark countryside.

He accelerated into the unmarked Curve. The Edsel rolled on its springs, tires pounded against fender wells. Canted into The Curve he saw, first, the skid marks that stretched into the night, and, second, the cloud of dust that hung in the air, slowly drifting north: another car for Inner's cornfield.

In the field below The Curve, where the corn stalks jutted door-high, tail-lights were small red eyes. He angled his car to the road until headlights framed a curious vignette: the twenty-foot convertible, and beside it dressed in silver lame was Joanie, as if she were waiting for him.

"Shall I call *any* tow truck," he yelled, "or have you got Triple-A?"

"Couldn't you *pleaze—*"

Across the silent field he heard her exasperated moan, and she began to pick her way across the dark soil. A car roared through The Curve, tires squealing; at the crest its lights touched her and flicked on, into the night.

"Just a *teeny* pull," she said, climbing the slight bank, kicking black loam from her shoes to the pavement. "I'll make it worth your while—Oh, it's *you!*" She laughed and looked toward the car that sat like a mirage in the headlight beams. "I'm *reely* sorry about the other night. I gave Amphora hell for bouncing you. *Reely* I did."

"Not at all. It happens all the time."

"Then, please get me out of here."

"I can't do it with this, but I'll tell you what: I'll call the man who owns the field."

"Oh, hell," she said, surveying the distance between the Edsel and her car. Her toe flicked out to kick at the road's shingle. "It's not the money—it's the law. If a screw comes past I'll get my license suspended—*again.*"

Somewhere a motorcycle sliced the night with its brittle exhaust, perhaps leaving Hubert's (Open All Nite) Drive-Inn for The Point, and beyond the yellow light beams, beyond the crashed twenty foot convertible, in the marsh where Johnson Creek lapped the cornfield, the cry of frogs pulsated, lonely and mocking. In his anger, Mill was unwilling to do anyone a favor. In fact, the thought of leaving her on the roadside gave him sadistic pleasure. But when she said it was not the money, no indeedy, he knew he had her: he would dicker, and because he hadn't eaten since noon it would not need to be largely cash.

"I pull you out," he said, "You ask me to supper tonight. At your house."

"You're out of your gawddamn *mind,"* she said, stomping her foot, turning to again survey the distance.

"The county sheriff's patrol ought to be by here just any time now—"

Even when she agreed to his proposal, said that it was a deal, she refused to shake hands on it.

Mill backed the Edsel into the field and, with the length of drag-bucket cable his father always carried in the trunk, he linked the two cars, As if the first time was only a rehearsal, he and Joanie tore up rows of com stalks to pack under the rear wheels, and then, engines racing, wheels spinning in the black loam, they advanced to the road's edge.

Mill was coiling the cable into the Edsel's trunk when Joanie approached with the twenty, holding it well away from her. It was no deal—her fingers had been crossed—and he could *buy* his own dinner.

"Nosir, I would not," he said, hearing an echo of Fronty's stubborn words. "I had thought of a quiet meal at your place. Home cooking. Candles. A good wine."

Even as she threw the bill at him and turned toward the car, Mill was past her and had the ignition key in his raised hand, ready to cast it into the night.

A car flashed through the sickle-blade of The Curve and was gone, the lights catching for a second two people frozen in expressions of anger and pleading. A roadside domestic quarrel: it was Saturday night.

"Okay," she said, reaching for the key. "Okay, it's a deal." She admitted that perhaps she did owe him *something*–but this time he made her shake hands, as a binder.

Headlights flashed on the fragmented windshields of Inner's yard, and Mill followed her exhaust toward the city. She drove fast, trying to lose him; her tail-lights diminished into the empty night, and she was gone. He could not expect to win, but his loss would not be total. For when he had finished coiling the cable into the Edsel's trunk, as he slammed the lid he had noticed the paper beside his foot: the twenty dollar bill, which now rested securely in his jacket pocket.

He caught her at the stop light in Loaner's Comer. On the opposite comer waited a patrol car, its white door plainly visible. She did not want her license suspended *again.*

He followed the convertible's tail-lights down Foster until they came to Powell, and at the stoplight he could see Ron Something in the doorway of the tavern, waving his derby in the air and shouting. The light changed, the convertible turned left and with shrieking tires accelerated down Powell. Mill was close behind, a cloud of grey smoke swirling from the Edsel's exhaust.

Down Powell to the bridge, and as they crossed the Willamette the heart of the city unfolded in a blaze of neon: the clocks on the old *Journal* building tower, the huge public utilities sign, the square heights of office buildings; behind, forming one side of a natural bowl, steep hills were dark against the night sky.

It was into these hills that Joanie raced. From the end of the bridge they drove beside or under the unfinished arches, huge frames of concrete that stood like Roman ruins–a demolished aqueduct–and as their exhausts rumbled off the constructions Mill realized that he had not been this far from home since his return. He had scarcely been out of the neighborhood.

At south Broadway she turned right and Mill raced through on the yellow. As he closed the gap her brake lights flared once, and with no signal at all she swung left across traffic and up the hill to Vista. Uphill, past the medical school, and he followed her lights around every narrow, exclusive corner of the Heights. Except for the two speeding cars the tree-lined streets were quiet, like the peaceful, shady sets of old movies, where Ronnie Coleman smoked his pipe in a paneled den and the only real threat was gossip.

Through the arch of hedge he followed, an opening not much larger than that at The Place, and far up the baroque twist of asphalt he saw her brake lights flare and die. As he parked, Joanie was already up the steps and through the front door, the sweeping curve of her thigh emerging into the hard geometry of the door frame.

She was not in the hallway, nor in the huge room beyond. He listened for movement, the scrape of high heels against marble, but heard only the soft creak of the chandelier as it swayed in a slight breeze. Under this complexity of glass pendulums he waited, and when he looked away from the chain by which it was suspended, which disappeared somewhere in the high, dark ceiling, he noticed the room. It was vast, medieval: all walls were paneled in an oiled, glowing wood–ebony, perhaps–and divided by intricate leaded windows and heavy drapes. Everything–the dark, stern furniture, marble fireplace, the solid oak front door–seemed hand-made and had been built to endure. Two large paintings broke the spectrum of dark hues in the room—a Brueghel and a Vermeer, and he was certain that they weren't copies.

Joanie came from a side door, breathless, as if she had just concealed something. Instead of the silver dress she wore a skirt and sheer white blouse. She stood by the fireplace, rubbing her hands together, then shrugged hopelessly and moved toward another door, saying: "Since you're here, have a drink. I'll start something."

"Don't trouble yourself. Something simple."

Mill was thinking of cold mutton or roast beef, whatever might be left over from the evening meal, when the door opened again. "By the way," she said, "I meant to ask the name of your tailor—that jacket's fantastic!" Her laughter spun out from the kitchen and rose to the dark heights of the room. Silently he cursed Ron Something, and Karl, and cursed himself for having pawned what few clothes he had once owned.

He found the liquor cabinet, poured an inch of Haig & Haig 5 Star into a glass, and took a cigar from the humidor. As he searched the room for a match, his fingers touched every surface—the smooth table facings, the china and brass lamp bases, the settee's black leather—with familiarity; when he heard a refrigerator door slam in the kitchen, he easily imagined that all this was *his,* that he did belong here, that he was lounging among his own vast spaces. From this house he didn't intend to be bounced.

He hefted a silver ashtray and considered its value. On tables and shelves were fine, rare objects, most small enough to fit in one's pocket. But something was wrong with the room, and as he lifted a porcelain figurine he saw its outline on the wood's surface. The room needed a good cleaning! Looking back, he saw the lines his fingertips had left.

An ornate chess set of carved jade was grouped for battle; the film of dust they stood in indicated that they had been mustered for some time. Then he noticed the lint balls on the elegant carpet, and that the brass fireplace equipment was badly tarnished, and he was puzzled.

He crossed the dusty room and faced the high ebony doors, wide enough to drive the Edsel through. He twisted the ornate knob, and one side of the panels swung silently into oily blackness. Tobacco, book must, the sweet smell of leather rushed out—the rich odor of sanitary decay—and when the door had opened fully the lights flicked on by some remote control.

The den was the size of a small tennis court. One wall was a bookcase, the volumes arranged by color: a rainbow of maroon, sienna, green morocco, and gold gilt. On the opposite wall was sporting equipment: crossed skis, fencing sabers, tennis racquets, and a glass-front gun cabinet. When he opened the sliding door below he found stacks of games: Monopoly, Bingo, decks of cards, a small roulette wheel. This was a sporting family, no doubt. There was a billiard table, and built around the massive fireplace were shelves of trophies: tiny ballplayers, runners, sail boats were mounted on gold pedestals.

But it was the private gallery of portraits over the trophies that he studied.

From the confines of the massive, detailed bronze frame a stem, dumpy man frowned; a large man, whose chin lacked strength, whose rosy cheeks were not jovial.

Beside him was not a painting but a snapshot or newspaper photo that had been blown up to four by eight. Mill could clearly see the texture of magnified dots, which looked like dirty pores on the hammy faun face that grinned from behind the wheel of an open Cadillac. Across the fender and hood lay a shattered goal post, and in the background, like extras on the set of an old movie, were throngs of people waving hip-flasks and Yale pennants.

Mill studied this curious tableau, and when he moved to the next painting, his heart staggered. The young man wore a red racing jacket and sat in the cockpit of a silver Grand Prix car. Even though the man wore a crash helmet and goggles which hung below his chin, to Mill it was like looking in a mirror: the long, slightly crooked nose, the high cheekbones, the thin lips. If under the helmet the man's hair should be primer black, and if his eyes were a half-tone lighter blue, he and Mill might pass for brothers.

Suddenly he recalled the instant at The Place when Joanie had been serious, when she had cut off her line of nonsense to stare at his face she had said that Mill reminded her of someone she had known.

"Found your way about, I see..."

Mill lifted his shoulders, swirled his drink, and said nothing as she slowly crossed the room, her arms folded tightly under her breasts. She sat on the edge of the billiards table. "All my wonderful family."

She motioned to the first portrait. "This pompous ass is Uncle Rathbone. A provision of the will."

"The will?"

"It states that I have to keep his mirthless visage in every house I own—in memoriam. But there's the money."

"Money?"

"Most of the family wealth descends from him. His first mill was at the junction of the Clackamas and Willamette, and he could float his logs down both of them. By the time he'd stripped the hills bare he had enough money to expand his holdings and with the help of some politicians he acquired a shipyard—that was handy during the war."

She moved sideways, to stand before the enlarged photo of the man in the open Cadillac. "That's Daddy. In one of the great moments of his life—Yale beat Harvard and Daddy drove onto the field and smashed the goal posts down. All our family has been keen on games, sports, the spirit of competition—of dammit, *winning*. But I guess Daddy was the keenest. After all, he had no need to make money, it was already made. Scads of it. But even if he didn't compete in the business world, he did do one constructive thing—he invented a quick-snap catch, for brassieres and such—and made another fortune. They used a lot of them during the war. Uncle Rathbone thought Daddy was simply playing around in the basement!

"Poor Daddy, he was the happiest when he'd go back to the little tavern of his college days. He'd have a couple of beers and when he was the center of the crowd he'd cry *Yeah Yale!* and with a mighty jump he'd smash the ceiling with his head. They loved it. Then, covered with lath and plaster, he'd pay damages and stand drinks."

Mill was amazed—in this huge hall, below the portraits, a drink, a beautiful woman smiling at his amazement—was she putting him on? "Where is he now?"

"Dead. He and Momma were killed in a plane crash when I was eight. Uncle Rathbone raised my brother and I. This," she said, motioning to the young man in the Grand Prix car, "is my brother, Tony. Needless to say, with a name like Tony Maloney he was an expert boxer. And a good football player, although he was too light, really. I guess he wanted to be like the Daddy he couldn't remember."

Mill searched the face of the young aristocrat—a modern Dick Seaman, quick, clever, rich, schooled in several languages. A gentleman of the sport, who need not work on cars but only drive them the very best he could. Mill searched the face frozen beneath the shell of varnish—and saw an almost exact reflection of his own.

"Where's he?"

"Dead. They're all dead."

"Racing?" Mill asked. He had to know any fragment of the short history of Joanie's brother, who so closely resembled him; this boy whose death had left Joanie sole heir to a fortune. He had to know because his purpose in this house was to get Joanie to invest in the Sports Special. But how could he mention the racing car if her brother—

"Not exactly," she said. "Well, not in the race itself, but in the pits. He was underneath, working on the car, and it's the craziest thing—the jack slipped."

Deep in Mill's stomach something recoiled and his eyes slowly turned from the portrait to the girl, to see if she was

75

joking—frame by frame the bizarre anecdotes accumulated, and he was wondering whether *any* of them could be believed. But her face mirrored the tragedy, and in the wealth of this room her lips quivered without tears: *It's not how you play the game, dammit* he could imagine her father saying, *it's winning!* He wanted to cross the room to hold her tightly, but even as he put down his empty glass and took a step forward she was moving away. "The dinner. It'll burn," she said, running from the den, through the giant room and beyond, her high-heels a sharp patter against the marble and wood.

Mill took one last look at the room and pulled the door closed; as the lights extinguished automatically he knew that he could say nothing about the Sports Special.

"Dammit. I can't cook."

When she put the tray on the coffee table Mill saw why she had tried to dissuade him from coming for dinner: two TV dinners steamed in their original tinfoil wrappers, beneath the artist's multi-colored rendering of meat, potatoes, and vegetables. A boat-shaped wooden bowl held chopped lettuce, without dressing, and beside it were two paper cartons of yogurt. In the center of the tray was a magnum of Mumm's No.1 Cup. "I let all the servants go last January."

Not cold mutton nor roast beef, but a grey meat patty, adhesive mashed potatoes, hard peas. Mill grabbed the plastic fork and ate with a genuine hunger. Now he knew why she had protested on the road, why dust collected in the absence of servants, why an air of sanitary decay flowed from room to room—why, she was *lonely,* no doubt she lived in a single room of this great house, ate TV dinners alone, and jumped into that twenty-foot convertible to roam the city hoping to escape from her past. Across from him Joanie balanced the tray on her knees, and strong jaws chewed with enthusiasm. She ate in silence, and put her tray down only once to open the champagne—her fingers worked the cork deftly, there was a solid pop, like an acetylene torch being turned off, but almost no overflow. She was familiar with champagne, and Mill imagined the small girl opening a row of bottles for her Daddy in the den, as they played Easy Money.

Too soon the dished tinfoil compartments were empty, and Joanie threw the wrappers in the fireplace. She crossed the room to start the stereo. The record was classical, and the heavy, dirge-like music was appropriate to the huge room it filled, although Mill would have liked something snappier.

She returned, her walk a series of athletic motions, and sat on the sofa, legs crossed, a cigarette in hand.

Drunk, in his slanting mind he saw his hand slip across her flat expanse of lap, over the smooth ungirdled flank, up the cage of waist that unwound in a widening upward spiral. He saw her nude, as naked as the calendar girl on the wall of Inner's dark cave (caption: 'Do you work on bodies?') and he saw the two of them alone in the rambling mansion, spending weeks sporting in each game room. Afterward they would shower and, wearing only fragrances, dine on TV dinners and champagne.

The silence was broken suddenly by both voices, lips moving in unison: "Why are you living here, alone?" and "Why are you working in that funny place?" They both stopped, then laughed—as if the questions had been prepared all evening.

"Well?" she said.

"Funny place? You mean Fronty's?" Finishing his drink, he poured another and gave her as honest an answer as he could. "It's a job. I like to keep things simple."

"Lord, I don't suppose anything could be more simple. But," she laughed, "I imagine it has compensations: the view must be awfully good from the windshield, in these days of short skirts."

What could he say? Tell her about the Sports Special, with the portrait of her dead brother hanging beyond that closed door? Tell her about Inner and Fronty, two old men;

about his family, poorer than church mice; about Tonto, Eddie—

"Okay. I'm escaping, shirking responsibilities. I could be a park attendant, spearing paper with a pointed stick."

"That's great," she said. "I mean, I think that's a wonderful attitude. Screw money. The noble savage. You're really a primitive, you know?" She lit another cigarette from the first and exhaled through her nose. "Turning wrenches. The *feel* of cold metal. Hands in grease. You really enjoy it."

"Cars happen to be what I know best."

"No, you *enjoy* machinery—as did Tony. He liked the way things fitted together."

"He did?" Mill was again surprised—that Tony, in the cockpit of the beautiful, bought Maserati, had had this sense of construction and that Joanie could know about it. "Okay, I do. I do like machines, certain kinds. The well-made, finely-crafted, and that means doing it yourself." He walked across the room and stood looking out the window. "It's impossible to find craftsmanship anymore; cars are built to last for three years, houses for fifteen, and it's cheaper to buy new shoes than to get old ones half-soled. Look here." He pointed to the city that spread below them in a thousand lights, reaching to the distant radio towers of The Point. At the base of their hill, like a sandbox operation, the lights of tiny bulldozers moved the earth. The half-finished overpass jutted into darkness like silver ruins. While he had been away, or hiding in Fronty's cave of a garage, day and night the pile drivers, cement trucks, an army labored to change the city. While he worried about the city's margins, or a restless population pushing out the city's limits, the interior was being systematically destroyed.

"Look at that. The most beautiful part of the city is being leveled for a lousy freeway. I can remember fifteen or twenty years ago, when—"

"That's progress."

"Toward what?" he asked, pacing the floor before the window. "Toward what? In ten years this city will be so screwed up—I mean, it scares me. The whole continent paved coast to coast, and poorly done at that." His pace quickened in the limited circle, and as he talked he could feel the tic begin to tug under his cheek. "An exploded population anchored to the mortgages of a billion jerry-built houses, which fall around their heads. A land of super-markets, shopping malls, parking lots—everything leveled, paved with asphalt—"

"That's called change. You get more people, they need houses, stores—"

"That's fine, up here in the high rent district. You can look down on that urban renewal disaster area; they'll never build a McDonald's or a Taco Time in your front yard."

"Maybe a high-rise? I'm thinking of selling."

He wheeled, faced her, and could not tell if she was serious. "You're kidding, right. You wouldn't sell. Look at this place." He stomped across the room, banged his fist on walls, tables, the marble fireplace. "It's *built,*" he said. "Built to last." In desperation he collapsed on the couch, and filled his glass. "Would you?"

"I sure would," she said, picking up the ashtray that he had knocked over. "I don't give a damn what becomes of this house—or this city. I live here because I'm here, and I live alone because I want to. Next week I just might fly to Athens, and if you think I'll be worrying about whether the Parthenon will fall over, you're crazy."

"Blow it up or pave it over—ahhh, this is an impossible world."

"And that," she said, sitting beside him, "is what makes it fun. Be a realist; some problems you can't dent."

"Exactly what I'm doing," he said. "Keeping things simple—responding only to earth, air, fire, and water."

"Good boy. *Now* I'm interested in you again."

"But you wouldn't really, would you?" He looked toward the dark paneled walls, the marble, the perfectly joined beams that supported the high ceiling—and he trembled, imagining the wrecker's ball swinging its weight into the solid old walls. Over its foundation he saw the high-rise apartment house, a massive growth on the city's skyline.

"Let me have a cigarette," he said.

She took two from the teakwood box on the table, and handed one to him. But as the cigarette lingered in the air, he took the hand that offered it—felt the tapered strong fingers flex under his, the hand clench slightly. When she smiled he let the cigarette fall to the floor and his free hand moved slowly to her neck, pulling her to him. When he had asked her for the cigarette he had not known that he would kiss her, but now her face was large and vague before his and their lips touched. His breath escaped; he was thinking of the dust, the echoes of empty rooms, of TV dinners, of how *lonely* she was in this aging abandoned house.

The lips on his were incredibly soft, but unparted, unparting. He felt her arms around his neck; against his hands her hair, silk, the shoulder blade's ridge, the bra strap. His tongue touched the lips rotating on his, prying at them. Her mouth stayed closed, although her breath came fast and tight fingers locked at his collar. Against his ribs pressed the bra's hard plates, and he was suddenly aware of the odor of lilacs.

His left hand eased from her back, slid under the arm and along the hollow. She did not resist as he followed the line that swooped down and sharply upward, giving the breast form, nor did she break the long kiss while his hand cupped hard against her—even after their lips separated she did not move away, head resting against his shoulder.

He undid the first buttons of her blouse. "Let's not do that," she said.

Top button, second—he saw the roll of flesh that disappeared into cleavage—and as his hand began to slide under cloth to tease the hard nipples, she took his wrist. "No," she said.

"Oh c'mon," he said, pulling back. "Christ, why not?"

His free hand slid toward the blouse's V, the silk almost as soft as the hot skin underneath. "What the hell."

"I said no."

Her grip tightened; then she grabbed his other hand, forcing it back, and held in place by this woman he felt something far away in his head begin to stretch, threaten to snap. "Jeezus, look this could be beautiful. Y'know?" His fists rotated before his eyes, attempting to escape the strong fingers, and he said: "Beautiful. Y'know?"

Then one hand went dead. Her fingers dented the cords on his wrist—some small, secret pressure point which, when pressed, deadened the limb: a trick her Daddy had taught her.

"Damn you," he screamed, although there was no pain. "I'll—" and the next thing he knew he was on his back on the floor behind the couch. From the sitting position she had used her arms and one knee to lever him through the air and before the syllables had fallen from his lips the high dark ceiling swirled at him and away.

It's not how you play the game—

"I'm sorry," she said, laughing, fingers touching her mouth, while he sat in a ball rubbing his head. *"Reely,* I am." She bent to help him up, breasts spilling from the opened blouse, and once on his feet he held tightly to her arms, locking them to her sides. His mouth was against hers; his right hand released her arm and moved behind her, holding her elbow and forcing it behind her back. His body blocking her movement, his hand darted into the blouse.

—it's winning, dammit!

Instantly, he was again in the air, moving across the room.

The chandelier was a flash of icicles across his eyes as he flipped, and unwillingly he was running, carried by his own momentum. She had stepped away, turned her back, and when the arm he had pinned was flexed forward she had grabbed his wrist with both hands; shifting her hip slightly, she had flipped him. The deft movement had been so quick that he had no idea how it had been done until later, when he was running crazily across the room, arms out to grab any anchor: *she is stronger*–and when his legs struck the big leather chair, to send him sprawling into a heap beside the fireplace, his surprise was complete.

He held his head–going for Cloud Nine–and heard a sound like rushing water; opening his eyes he saw her standing where he had stood, laughing.

Quickly, as if he had only stumbled, he got up and shook himself. Walking toward that elaborate front door, he grabbed his jacket and entered the night air. His right sleeve hung free from the jacket body, and he slipped out of it, then tore off the other sleeve and threw them on the seat of the Edsel.

Behind him laughter boiled into the darkness, and just before he sped down the long driveway he heard her shout: "I don't even know your name!"

Down the tight curves of the baroque driveway and headed downhill, into the city, he whipped the wheel, the car whistling through the night over the narrow road. Crossing the Willamette he saw far to the southeast the high, beckoning fingers of the radio towers–at their base was The Point, that dark promontory where lovers were now grappling in backseats. He still had the twenty dollar bill Joanie had thrown to the ground; he considered finding a prostitute–that would be fine irony, he thought. Then he remembered Doretta K.'s phone number in his pocket, but could he arrive wearing a sleeveless jacket?

At the same instant he thought of Eddie, and it did not matter at all if she were Tonto's girl.

Straight home he drove and parked the Edsel in the street. In the front room he slipped past his father, asleep in his old chair before the TV's acetylene light, and silently climbed the stairs. He threw off the ruined jacket, dropped his slacks, shirt, worn necktie in a pile, and from the dresser he got a pair of Tonto's black puchuko pants and a white tee-shirt. The pants were tight at the crotch and the shirt bound under his arms–he felt squeezed into some kind of a *uniform,* as he stood feet apart in tennis shoes, a black leather cap pulled Iowan his head, hands in tight gloves.

"I'm cold."

When he slipped into the hallway he heard voices from the bathroom. Whatever words his mother said were lost in the noise of running water, but he heard Granny's voice clearly: "I'm *cold.* I'm so *cold."* Silently he moved downstairs, through the kitchen, where the clock read eleven-thirty. What the hell was Granny doing up, he wondered. He raised the garage door quietly, and even as the roadster's engine caught he let out the clutch, moving in reverse down the driveway. Without warming the engine he raced through the streets of sad, dark houses.

Straight to Hubert's (Open All Nite) Drive-Inn he drove, to park in the very center.

The lot was filled on this Saturday night. Silver bumpers were a continuous ribbon nosed into the neon lights; radios coughed the top ten hits in unison. Somewhere among the kids, among the backseat lovers, was Eddie.

In the center he braked to a stop and violated the city ordinance posted over the door: the horn rapped three times. Full-race radios were toned down; car by car a silence fell on the cluttered parking lot as faces were wrenched toward the roadster. They had seen it at the station, sitting— but here it was among them, and they listened to the *whomp whomp whomp* of the idling engine, the big cam's rough overlap.

Again Mill honked, impatient, daring someone to throw him off the lot; he almost hoped Gus or Marty would emerge from the shadows, for tonight he would not be stopped.

It was Eddie who came through the swinging doors, and when he hooked a thumb at her she came, laughing, moving in a crazy traffic dance of rolling hips and bouncing breasts.

"You want car service?"

"You bet," he said. *"That* is just what I want."

"Well, you're blowing, man. I heard the cry of the wild goose—and the wilder the goose, I always say—"

"Get in."

"Indeedy," she said, crossing his headlights and sliding across the ribbed leather; the door slammed of its own fragile weight when Mill accelerated to the end of the parking and was over the apron, tires squealing, into the street. He stepped the gas to the floor and the wind rushed at them, sweeping Eddie's hair into the slipstream.

"Wow, boy, you are with it tonight," Eddie said, gathering her hard, angular body tightly in the cockpit. "You. Are. With. It."

"Man," he said. "Call me *MAN.*"

"Whooooeeee—like prove it." Her hand slid over to hold the sleek chrome shaft of the gear lever.

At the first stop light he took a long look. His eyes held the point where the sickle shape of her chin and neck met the deep V of her blouse—the cloth was filled with an outward thrust now cast in red from the traffic light, hard and solid as bearing steel.

"Dragsville," Eddie said, spotting the car coming alongside them.

The Chev was brand new, just off the dealer's floor. The front end had been lowered until the car assumed the posture of speed, the forward slanting stance of competition. The four boys grinned as the driver stabbed the gas, the engine rising and falling beside this old A-Model roadster—and hadn't the salesman guaranteed their car would hit a hundred and thirty?

"Well now then there, kids," Mill said, trying to imagine how Tonto would say it. "Yass indeedy. I'm glad you painted that dog green—to hide in the grass, you know?"

On the seat he could feel Eddie bouncing. The roadster humped at a rough idle, the rhythm of sex currents.

Four grins faded. When the light changed Mill feathered the gas, moving slowly, then mashed it: the roadster jumped forward as the Chev fishtailed, tires spinning in lost traction.

The Chev moved to the roadster's rear fender, began to pull alongside. The tach was red-lined at seventy-five hundred when Mill threw a shift to second, all his fury and frustration exploding as his arm rammed the lever forward.

"Go gooooooooooo," Eddie screamed, hair blowing in lines of motion, as the Chev fell behind.

And who did she cheer? he wondered.

Ahead the light snapped yellow, red, but Mill had his foot to the floor and he was over before cross-traffic could move; he heard the Chev panic-stop, brakes locked.

His foot stayed on the gas until the radio beacons blinked above them in a light haze; nor did he slow for the turnoff too late to watch for cops now, and Mill found he didn't care—skidding in a long controlled drift toward the ditch until the big rear tires accepted power, gained traction, and the car was straight on the road, upright, and speeding into the slate-black night toward The Point, up the steep strip of asphalt.

"You won, man," she screamed, her hollow mouth cupped to his ear.

And the prize? he wondered. His foot was hard on the gas through the arching curve that crossed the upper reaches of the cemetery; he slowed slightly where the pavement ended and the road was gravel over twin ruts. When the roadster's grill reached the base of the radio beacons he stopped, pulling the car onto a short side road nearly covered with brush. Over his shoulder he saw a full moon rising, silhouetting the lonesome pine trees; below them was the sugar sparkling glaze of the city's lights.

"Whoooeee," she said, "that was a ride." His arms reached across the short space, pulling her to his side of the cockpit. One hand was on her back, the other circled her waist, and he felt the hardness of her bra under his fingers; felt shoulder muscles tense as she held back from his enclosure.

But as his hand moved upward to squeeze the base of her neck she relaxed, and leaned into him, her mouth slightly open. Under his other hand her waist contracted and he sensed the shudder of air exhaled involuntarily over their tongues. Her head rocked sideways against his—a style she had learned from the movies, and when she released him her head fell back on his arm, her breath heavy and fast through open lips, her blouse rising. Mill's hand caressed her waist, moved across her tight flat stomach, and in the silence of passion she took his hand and placed the fingers around her breast. The cup was angular, like metal plates, and when Mill opened the first button of her blouse she did not resist. He opened her to the waist, felt the arched curve of her flesh above the bra, and when he slipped the strap down the cup dropped. In the moonlight he could see the line that divided her tanned skin from the area protected by a bathing suit, and his finger traced across the white skin, to the black circle that was the nipple—in his hand her breast was large and hard, tilted upward without the bra's support, and yet when he touched the nipple he felt some inner mechanism click, felt the breast stiffen. Under the hardness at hand he felt his heart racing against ribs. His tongue passed across her hot skin, and his teeth crimped lightly on the nipple—instantly her arms were around his head, pulling him into her, and her tongue was probing his ear, entering, and as he was trying impossibly to get the whole breast into his mouth her hips began to move against the leather, rotating in motions his tongue followed, until she stiffened, and pushed him away.

She fell back, mouth open, and when his hand attempted to caress her thigh, she said, "No, don't."

All the frustration that had been building—the Fronty/Inner conflict, the crummy gas station which Fronty would not modernize, the aborted Sports Special, the battle he had lost with Joanie—emerged, and he furiously grabbed her wrists, holding them together with one hand while the other worked frantically, ripping cloth, sending buttons spinning into the darkness.

"Bastard!" she said, fighting against his assault; then she began to sob, a sound like the dim rattle of distant traffic, but even this display of emotion could not stop him. "You bastard!"

Chapter 7

Sunday morning, and in the mirror he saw Eddie's lipstick smeared over a wide area around his mouth; he soaked a corner of the towel in hot water to rub it off. He had wanted to return home and keep life simple. Marty and Gus would be telling Tonto the details: *Sheeut yes, he parked her at The Point.*

He shaved and as he came downstairs he heard Tonto's car roar off, the tailpipe clattering like the little gears in Mill's head. The house was empty. The Sunday paper lay unopened on the kitchen table and the coffee pot was cold. Nor did he see anyone in the back yard, as he walked shakily into the August heat toward the garage. Carefully he ran his fingers over the roadster's flanks; except for a few rock chips the car had not been damaged.

He had not believed her when she had claimed she was a virgin. Bad enough, he thought, that she was Tonto's girl. Now, in daylight, he could not reconcile the two images he had of Eddie: the hard-hipped traffic dancer of the drive-in, who got tough boys to do her bidding, and the virginal girl-child who had fought to resist him last night at The Point. *You bastard,* she had repeated, as he ripped off her clothes, *you're gonna pay.*

And he knew he would.

He was standing in the yard when the Edsel rocked to a stop. His mother emerged first, stooping, the black dress reflecting in the sunlight the area scuffed shiny over her hips and backside. "Oh Millard. Granny's taken from us!" She leaned against disaster, ready to fall, until her husband gently steered her into the house. "She passed on, Millard. Late last night."

They had been to the funeral home and then to church, and his mother's dramatic account of the tragedy indicated she had already told it several times: Granny had been walking the hallway, crying that she was *cold,* and insisting on her Saturday night bath. She had had one earlier, but she wouldn't go to sleep and therefore Mill's mother had dipped her quickly in the tub. She had left the room "only for a minute" to get a towel, and the old woman had plugged in the electric heater, which had somehow fallen into the bath water. Died instantly, the mother repeated, as if this were a small island of comfort in a sea of tragedy. She had felt no pain, whatsoever.

I'm so cold he had heard when he slipped upstairs to change into Tonto's clothes; she must have pulled the heater into the tub about the time he had held Eddie, feeling the warm bare breast under a swirling starry sky.

He didn't know what to say: Granny passing like a shade in a blue flash and a cloud of smoke as the house lights dimmed. Her eyes fogged over like blown fuses. Ashes was what the coroner had taken to the funeral home.

"If only I hadn't left the room," his mother said, reaching back to alter death. "If only I had watched her."

Tuesday, after the funeral, he got the first phone call.

From the cemetery he drove straight to Fronty's, and changed from his stiff blue suit into hot coveralls. The August air was sticky with heat and Mill cursed as he worked on a '38 International pickup—cursed every stubborn rusted nut, cursed the sweat binding the coveralls to his skin. Now he remembered how scorching days like this, or those when a winter wind swept from the Columbia Gorge through the open door, had changed his mind about becoming a journeyman mechanic. Those discomforts had sent him toward college. He had wanted to sit at a clean, polished desk and to wear a white shirt.

Fronty called him to the phone, and as Mill rolled the Jeeper's Creeper from under the truck he cursed the heat and the dust which fell from fender wells into his hair, ears, neck, the abrasive mud against his sweaty back. He remembered now why he had hated the garage: there were too many days when it seemed a kind of death, the lube pit a stuffy tomb, skinned knuckles a slow bleeding—a burial almost as real as the one earlier today on the hill.

The funeral had been simple: a small clump of bouquets with big ribbons from the neighbors; a grey cloth-covered coffin housed the fragile remains. His mother had wanted Granny to have a large headstone, with an epitaph and carved angels, but there was no money for that kind of thing.

Mill had stood before the open hole, the fresh dark dirt already baking in the hot August sun, and as the minister spoke the last words Mill looked down—across the golden reservoir, where water-dogs flicked lazily; across the rows of blazing white crosses that marked the military dead; to Foster Road, where he could see Inner's yard spreading to the fallen back fence, every wrecked auto a kind of death marker, and around The Curve where Fronty rolled his chair toward the island. The old neighborhood spread at his feet like a map, and he could see every change. The sermon had ended, the casket was being lowered and Mill had looked up the side of the mountain to a final promontory, The Point; around that single pine the grass would be still beaten flat. There he and Eddie had fought, about the same time Granny had taken the heater into the tub.

Mill scrambled from under the pickup, wiped his hands and took the phone from Fronty. "Yeah?"

"Mill baby?"

He had expected Joanie. But this anonymous voice was low and husky; he thought of Gus or Marty. Then he thought of Amphora, the gorillas at The Place, and their warning that if he ever saw Joanie again he would get *burned*.

"Man, you have had the meat."

Mill, startled, tried to think of something clever and defiant, like *You bet, man, I had it Saturday night,* but against his ear he heard only the insistent dial tone.

He hung up the phone, and seeing in his mind's eye that mail-order pistol, that orchid colored coupe that patrolled his street, he was suddenly afraid. His throat was dust, and the hand which replaced the receiver trembled. If he had

had no feelings about Granny's death on Sunday, today the funeral had a sobering effect: death stopped the system, ended life as surely as the wrecks in Inner's yard were stopped, to bleed rust into the ground. In the end all were totaled.

He took a warm Coke from the machine, to clear his throat. In the shade of the wooden canopy Fronty sat upright in his wheelchair, staring across the shimmering gravel of the parking area as if estimating the property's value. Again Mill asked the question: "Would you please just take a look, please?"

"Nosir, I would not."

"Only to look?"

"Nosir! I have not been around that corner for—"

Perhaps the Sports Special did not really matter anymore. The frame rails were finished, and yesterday he had blocked in place an Offy engine from one of Fronty's midget race cars. In another week, if they had any money, he could order sheet aluminum and start constructing the body templates. First, however, he needed those Alpha parts.

Perhaps the Sports Special was not important anymore. But Inner and Fronty were; this morning, when he had stood in the cemetery and looked down at the map that unfolded at his feet, he knew the old men had to be brought together, he had to resolve their feud. Mill told himself it was his *duty*. He could not let those old men go to their graves filled with hate simply because they were stubborn.

There were two more calls that afternoon. And calls the next day, and again on Thursday. At first he was sure the callers—for there were different voices—were Eddie's friends: they sounded young, eager, nervous, and always added the epithet *man*. They said, *Check yore balls man cause we gonna cut;* before the dial tone buzzed he heard in the background a wild, whooping laughter. Another time the voice said: *We keeping this rusty blade for you man.* But at times

91

he was not so sure it wasn't Amphora and his gorillas: *Play with fire you get burned.* And later he was almost certain: *We're going to let your air out.*

Mill would hang up the receiver, arms heavy and weak, the sweat inside his coveralls suddenly cold. Fronty began to look at him in a strange way, and Mill knew the old man wondered why Mill hung up without speaking, and so Mill began to invent monologues to the dial tone, as if he were being interviewed for the Big Job. Thursday the calls came more often, and it seemed to Mill that he spent half the day answering the phone. On Tuesday he had felt a stab of fear but by Thursday he was scared, his nerves gone, his mind worn from fear and a lack of sleep. For he had not gone home since the morning of the funeral. Tuesday night, after Fronty had hand shifted his pickup in to the dark, Mill had decided to stay in the station; he had pulled the roadster inside and slept on the backseat of a customer's car. The rest of the week he stayed in the garage at night and ate his meals at Gee-Eye's cafe. But sleep was impossible; he dozed, fully awake at the roar of any car shooting down Foster into the night, or went to the window as imaginary footsteps sounded beside the garage. Running to the window, he watched shadows melt into dawn.

Any sleep, when it came, was the sleep of exhaustion. Always he dreamed: the gray landscape, broken trees, the heavy oil smoke hanging in the air. Fragments of chrome and glass littered the ground. Across this stretched two lines of strange people chained ankle to ankle; in unison the rows of ten pound sledge hammers fell.

By Friday morning the front of his skull was numb, and all through his body, like a wiring diagram, electric currents twitched. During breakfast he kept one hand on his cheek, so Gee-Eye could not see the nervous tic that pulled the jaw into a fictitious smile. And after every phone call the chiaroscuro of death hazed his mind—he saw Granny's grave, Inner's wrecking yard, the finality of death.

The sun was a magnet pulling the day toward noon when Fronty's ancient truck rolled across the dusty apron, to park in the small panel of shade at the side. Mill watched his arm throw the crescent wrench across the room, and felt his legs walk across the pump island, past the bench where Snuff dozed, and directly to the truck. The old man had lowered himself into the wheel chair, when Mill yelled: "Will you listen to reason?"

He was not a hard man, really, so he folded his arms and dropped his head, a foetus in the chair–fading under the incessant torment of this crazed, red-eyed boy.

"Well?" He looked at Snuff, as if the conversation was between them.

"You must go there and dicker. Inner will settle for nothing less."

"Nosir–"

"Then I'm through," Mill yelled. "I don't have to stay here. Tomorrow night I'll get my pay and I'm heading for California–for the Big Job."

"Wait," Fronty said, pulling Mill back from the four angry steps he had taken.

Fronty did not move for a long time. Then he rotated the chair in one slow revolution, as if surveying the diurnal business of years one last time. He exhaled a vicious blast of air, wheeled to the pickup, and suspended by one arm from the roof he folded the chair neatly with a practiced motion and dropped it in the bed. He fiddled with the hand controls–devices he had designed himself after his accident, for this truck that he would never allow to be painted company colors–and he said: "Watch the station, Snuff."

There had been a certain levering force applied here, as a rusty nut breaks under the purchase of a wrench or a nail is clawed from wood, to get Fronty into his truck. Mill's heart was pounding as he waved to Snuff and climbed on the hay-filled seat.

"I haven't been there for thirty years," Fronty mumbled. He pulled the hand clutch toward him, stroked the gear lever forward, and eased the gas handle back. They were moving.

To Inner's yard. Mill couldn't believe it.

"Was it cars?" he asked.

"No," Fronty said. Back on the clutch handle, into second with the floor shift, steadily back on the gas lever. "A woman." His eyes slid to Mill, then to the road. "Surprised that old men ever had time for the women? Little girl who lived in a big house near the tracks. Right over there."

Where Fronty pointed the pitched red roofs of tract houses sprouted through the trees—prolepsis of the city moving past its limits.

"House is gone now," Fronty said. He dropped to third gear and when the clutch engaged his hand strayed to the sun visor and turned it down, as if tipping his hat: what he handed Mill was a weathered yellow-tint photo of a girl whose long unwinding curls framed a flat china doll face.

Mill studied the picture in silent amazement. Fronty and Inner, good friends who loved the same girl. As he looked at the picture he heard the story. The pressure built, and they fought—Mill saw them stripped to the waist in that open field, over there, fighting with bare knuckles. Not a movie fight, but a mean no holds barred three day battle under the blazing sun and through the long nights—a battle of giants.

"Always thought it was a draw. Course Inner claimed he'd won, so I said I had. Old Inner never forgot, and he never found another woman—he's *stubborn*."

The confession was quick; they were already in the yard. Mill wanted to ask a million questions but Fronty was busy with the hand controls, working brake and clutch and gas, the truck weaving through the maze of rusting metal. Before them the Alpha coupe was a blaze of red sinking into weeds. Fronty's useless feet touched the running board as his hand reached into the bed and easily sprung open the chair, like a man opening an umbrella.

"We can use the suspension," Mill said. "Transmission. Rear end."

"At least." Fronty was admiring the simple, competent construction of the foreign machine when the mighty roar of indignation came from behind them.

"What're you fellers doing messin' around?" Inner tugged at his fly, squared the greasy skullcap on his gnome head; his hands sneaked to his hips and he hunched his shoulders. "You read the signs?"

"I don't see no trees passing."

"Up yours, funny boy. Collich boy. This is a bisiness." But he relented his intimidating pose, and leaned on the rusted cowl of a Model A Ford. He yanked off a long piece of summer grass and stuck it between his yellowed teeth, like a curious goat dancing in a rusty tree.

Across from him Fronty sat erect, his hands tinkering with the chair's spokes.

He's blushing, Mill thought. Perhaps he realizes they are no longer two boys, fighting for love. Or had he known that long ago?

"What yer want, messin' around?"

"Hell, you know what we want," Mill said.

"Mr. McMahon." Before any argument could begin Fronty's voice interrupted them, and his words were directed to the man he had not spoken to for thirty years. "To the point, because I know you're busy: we wish to utilize some of this car, to build a Sports Special. To win the big Grand Pree money. Now, old men shouldn't stand in the way of youth, and to be business like you will be a third partner."

"A third of nothing," Inner hissed.

"We'll pay you two-thirds of what you paid for this car, and you'll own one-third of the finished racer."

But Inner wanted more than business and dickering—he wanted satisfaction. The thirty year feud gnawed at his spleen every morning, and every meal he had to cook reminded him of the woman he had lost. Fronty knew the old feud was at stake, and so he spoke the words that made Inner throw off his skull cap and stomp it into the dry baked earth. Mill sucked in the heat of the day, for surely the deal was off now—and Inner had been half-convinced.

"You silly old crow bait," Fronty taunted. His eyes wandered over the yard where it seemed an ancient giant traffic jam had fallen into a hundred years' sleep.

Inner roared and stomped the baked earth, then stilled his savage dance with a gesture of contrition that amazed Mill; he extended his hand. (Possibly only to pick up his hat, Mill realized later.)

Quickly, because he knew the junky pacified without strong-arm tactics would be an unforgiving; complaining, restless old man, Fronty said: "About that old score, we'll say you won. So that we may proceed. But I still know I'm the better man."

"The hell you say, you crippled kenmezzler." He followed the unintelligible obscenity with a savage scream, like a shaft seizing.

Fronty threw off the upper half of his coveralls, tied the sleeves around his waist, and raised himself from the chair to place his right elbow on the flat roof of the car. "Two out of three."

The Model A Ford was wheel less, windowless, running board deep in mud and overgrown with grass, and the roof level was just elbow high. When Inner came around the other side and flung the rusted door that came off in his hand halfway to the road, skimming it like a rusty sun across the sky, and walked into the seatless, glassless car body, it became a small empty room—an arena. He stood with his feet apart on the car floor, his head and shoulders rising above the cloth less top. Ripping his shirt off, he exposed grey underwear peppered with holes. A wave of sweat smell rose from the black yawning armpits. His face wore a look of dazed anger and his lips moved soundlessly, as if repeating over and over that he would win this time, for sure.

Inner propped his elbow at a right angle against the steel roof and they were ready. Their hands fitted together and slowly Mill counted to three.

Had Mill any money to bet, it would have been placed on Fronty. Over the years Mill had seen Fronty's legs atrophy, and his arms double in strength. Now the muscles swelled like high-dome pistons. Fronty's arms and shoulders were a pale aluminum to that distinct line at the wrists and the V of his throat where the skin was a wrinkled red. He seemed to be wearing a permanent old-fashioned swim suit.

Across from him Inner sucked air like a one-lung compressor. His curses rang across the yard, while Fronty was calm but working. Slowly arms wavered, left to right and back again, shuddering each time the apex was passed. Muscles and veins were near bursting. A distant thunder rolled across the sky as the steel under their elbows warped and buckled with stress. Sparks arced as two small cavities were worn in the metal; grease and oil melted from their hands under the heat of friction and collected in the dents, shiny tide pools.

Mill thought: Why, they were young men, in love, and fighting for love when that car they now lever over was new. They were young, and planning their lives. And neither figured to end up with a junkyard or a broken-down station. But then it had seemed possible to see money and a future in automobiles—like the radio or the new sound movies—so they stayed in this isolated patch of land where they are barely able to make a living.

Then, slowly, their arms toppled and fell: Inner's point.

Inner laughed, released Fronty's arm and rubbed the sweat from his grease crusted hands against his pants. "One more."

"Correction," Fronty said. "Two more."

Quicker this time, Fronty with quiet determination leaned against the car and kept his free hand outstretched, a rigger for balance. He sucked the hot air and almost without effort pushed Inner's arm against the blazing metal; he held it there and the two old men were for that second face to face, kissing close and tied for points.

The yard was silent except for the wheezing of two men near to collapse. No traffic slapped against the road outside and Mill could not hear the whine of giant saws or the whirr of Hysters at the lumber yard.

Elbows were fitted into the two grooves they had peened; claw hands slid together for this final lap.

Neither man gave an inch.

Mill was certain Fronty would win easily, but Inner strained, cursed, his temples raging, and in the terrible heat his face was the color of the rusted metal around him.

For half an hour they grunted, cursed, or hung motionless. Under their elbows came the cannonade of war as the metal buckled. Sweat poured, washed the dust from Inner's tattoos in grotesque patterns of color and mud. From the sun's heat and the friction of their hands the oozing grease ignited in the hot metal kettles at their elbows, then fizzled out as sweat ran down arms to extinguish the blaze. Inner went up on his toes, to blot the sun from Mill's view; Fronty countered by applying pressure, which threatened to topple the car. Already their struggle had forced it inches into the ground, opening a seismic land crack.

For half an hour Mill waited tensely not for a winner but a loser—the one who would misfire, burst a heart valve, and fall to the hot dusty yard in a row with the wrecked autos.

And for Mill the thought blazed like the noon sun that they *had* changed: they had been young in that once upon a time of the other fight, Fronty standing on two sturdy legs, Inner without the tire of weight above his belt—both men lean and peen-hammer hard with their punches. They had been young and in love, and the whole horizon of their future stretched ahead, limitless and golden.

Much later, when Fronty's hand came slowly down, to quickly touch the metal, Inner didn't see what Mill saw—a cautious smile on Fronty's face. The junky threw himself away, like a fighter against the ropes as he hung onto the wood ribs.

On the way back to the station, Mill said: "I was worried. That it would go on for another thirty years." There was silence until the gravel of the parking lot crumbled beneath the wheels and when it seemed that safety had been reached, Mill insisted: "You could have won. Easily."

Fronty began to protest, then flipped off the key and stared through the aged, yellow glass of the windshield. "Let Inner be beat by a hopeless cripple?" He suspended his weight against the door and lowered the wheelchair to the ground.

"It was that, or dicker."

Within the hour Inner brought the Alpha coupe to the station. His battered tow truck whined to a stop and Inner and Fronty went into the office to make the deal legal.

"Luff a moses," Snuff said, and finally he was making sense. "Ah niver taught ah'd seed dah day."

When Mill wanted to stay after work to tear the Alpha apart, Fronty said he would be staying alone. Yes, he and Margie had invited Inner and Snuff over, yes, to the house for dinner. Some good home cooking. Yes, it seemed a lousy way for a young man to spend a Friday night, dismantling a car.

Inner appeared at seven, his hair split in the center, like the yellow line on a wet slick highway. He wore a primer grey suit, and had the tufts of hair in his nose and ears trimmed to the limits of decency. But his scrubbed hands showed a roadmap of imbedded grease, his large nose pores were filled with a glazed sediment that was permanent.

"For Margie," he said. His hand held a clump of flowers picked from the auto graveyard.

Then they were gone. The three old men packed in the cab of Fronty's truck, and before third gear was reached Mill could hear them laughing, and Snuff singing. It was the howl of a burnt-out bearing.

Mill jacked the Alpha coupe onto stands, and began to remove the differential. Evening became night, and from the empty darkness he kept hearing noises—a twig breaking, cautious steps. Snuff had said that Mill had had two calls that afternoon, and Mill could imagine who they were from. He didn't want to be caught under the car, defenseless.

By nine he knew he couldn't stay at the station. He had to get out, if only to Grogan's for a warm, soapy beer; he had to escape the honey-dark grease and fuel odors that filled his lungs. What he really needed, he knew, was a good bath.

He read the pumps and locked them. In the lube room he threw the master switch, plunging the station into darkness. He felt his way to the front door, where he snapped shut the big Yale padlock. His back to the road, he heard the machinegun sound of gravel, a premonition of violence. He turned to face the blinding glare of headlights and saw the burst of fire. The bullet had already shattered the window above the lock when Mill threw himself on the ground, into the circus flash of lights—his skull exploded, and far away he heard the whirr of tires on the gravel.

He lay still, softly crying against the pain that pounded through bone. In panic he had lunged into the door jamb, and a large knot mounted near the part in his hair, growing under the hand that compressed his skull.

The bastards mean business.

He rose, stumbling, lights flashing between his eyes at every step. As he rested against the building gravel rumbled again, and he was caught in the glare of quad headlights. The car moved slowly toward him, the lights brilliant swirling circles tinged blue at the edges. Mill pawed the air, and as the lights swept through the full spectrum of colors he fell forward on the jagged, cutting gravel. Before he passed out he was silently laughing while he cursed Fronty for not making any improvements: he could at least have planted grass here.

Chapter 8

He is awakened to gun butts on his door by official men. In the confusion of midnight he offers what his hand holds: the title to his roadster.

His offer is apparently not what they want; heels click, belts slap, the men hum martial music. *Your papers are not in order,* one says, and he is ordered, in pajamas, into their official auto. On all sides they smell frankly of blood, of beatings, the authority of leather. Below the bills of caps they smile at his terror, each perfect tooth a headstone engraved with a question.

He has no answers. They ride the cobbled back-streets in silence, and he wonders Why? as they finger saps, play with the exquisite actions of automatics, exhale thin streams of evil cigarette smoke.

In the silence he is saved by a bell; the men all lean to the odometer, which has turned up four skulls. *Ahhhhh, a thousand,* says the driver. *Worn out.* He turns the corner and everybody transfers to a car whose ashtrays mirror newness. They drive off in this unused car, after one man has triggered the thermite bomb on the old front seat.

Later, the Judge says: *Thirty days or thirty thousand. Time is money.* His gavel smashes the bench as he speaks of over production, in an official way. *We need those parking spaces.*

But how much do we want? Mill is foolish enough to ask. How much do we need?

The Judge asks who does he think he is? Has he tried to find a parking place lately?

Who is he? A cobbler, concerned with lastings? Carpenter, mating the perfect bevels of edges? Or simply a citizen in pajamas ordered by official men into the night?

At 3 a.m., still in pajamas, he is chained by the ankle to a line, and armed with a sledge.

The chain stretches link by link between leg irons, linking a hundred people in two parallel lines across the barren landscape. A few jagged rocks push up from the earth's molten core, trees are leafless wrecks. The ground is decorated with fallen chrome, headlight rims, a broken antenna, a forgotten engine accessory sitting in grease, metal bleeding rust. Smoldering tires cast a pall across the floodlit field.

Twin lights glow at the far end of the line, and his neighbor, a heavy Negro woman, lifts her sledge. *Ah done paid the man fo ten years. Ah done got hit paid offn they come fo us both. Hit don't matter none ah cain't afford a new un.*

As her sledge is lifted overhead both breasts fall from her torn blouse. Her lips are wet with excitement, her eyes roll as the noise of steel rings closer. She moans some forgotten lyrics, hands gripping the sledgehammer tightly, every black muscle tense. The headlights have gone out but through the smoke Mill sees the glare of chrome, the fractured glass. The woman swings her sledge at a fender and the blow excites the air. The fender crumples lower, toward the tire, as the sledge careens downward into her knee. She shows no pain, and swings again.

A guard jabs Mill's back with his gun, and he swings his hammer overhead, sending concentric waves across the field. The deck lid crumples, shakes off paint, and the car continues to roll on its own wheels. His other neighbor, a teenage boy, swings his hammer in machined motions, the blows hitting like bullets.

The car limps on, bleeding oil, beaten hubcap high, rolls dazed to the waiting torch; in acetylene light it crumples to mere parts, a pool of pig iron.

Been here long? Mill asks.

Huh! the boy scoffs. *Six months—I aims to make it my life work. I'm good at it.*

Are they employing? Mill asks.

Huh! See those people in the smoke, unchained? They come here for the pay and the fun. That's what I aims to do.

You like this job?

Yeah, he says, leaning on the sledge, spitting. *It makes me feel good—right here—like I got power.*

A car coming from their end interrupts. Its lights blaze with newness. Its paint is barely scratched, its break-in oil unstained, its innocent body glows like a brochure. Under the fenders it harbors only a light dust, like peach fuzz.

But the hammers are not dazzled by the mysteries of metal.

The guards' whips crack past ears, guns probe backs. The sledges fall like rain across roofs, hoods, fenders, beating all hubcap high. And why, Mill wonders, is he swinging harder, with accuracy? Why does he want that magnificent machine demolished?

Ah done got hit paid offn they come fo us both, the Negro woman says, tucking her massive breasts behind tattered cloth.

I had mine all jazzed up, says the boy. *All new parts but they said it was too old.*

Lights come, dim through smoke. Mill sees his roadster idling along the barren landscape, feeble with age—no, it seems to bow, to beg his forgiveness, to be allowed to live its last days in some garage, or even in a wrecking yard.

The hammer drops from Mill's hand. He has created this car from parts, built it from junk; he knows and loves every intricate piece of its machinery. The roadster creeps forward and he is suddenly aware of the quiet. All along the chain the men and women wait in their shredded clothes, carboned skin, staring.

The roadster stops and the boy says: *They make you destroy your own. Then you're hooked. But you'll feel better, later.*

The hammer hangs heavy in his hands, until a gun nudges his back. *DESTROY IT!* the guard shouts. *DESTROY!* his fellow workers chant, hammers ready, eyes red with blood.

Something moves his hands upward, and the hammer falls. The car whimpers, but the body is barely creased; the old metal is strong, has integrity. There is no tinkle of tin. The car jerks ahead, moves into the falling hammers.

"My roadster!"

"I parked it in the garage—had a hell of a time starting it."

He felt a coolness against his cheek, a fast wind whipped around his head. Eyes parted slightly against the pain, he saw the tanned legs that tapered from the pedals to the leather upholstery; his face was pressed against the garnish molding and an eighty mph wind slapped his aching head. The convertible's top was down, and without moving he could see the stars fixed overhead in the blackest night possible. The damp air smelled of ferns and underbrush and moldy pine needles.

"Where are we?"

"Well, honey, you said you wanted to get out of town."

He did not remember saying that. In the center of his forehead the wind pressed against a blank spot the size of a steering wheel. Without moving his aching head he saw Joanie's white tennis shorts and the bulky knit sweater, the long legs that ended in heavy brown shoes, and the red rubber soles on the pedals had deep lugs like wide spaced teeth. She seemed to be dressed for some sporting event, and immediately he thought of California.

Tires hummed in his head, and the car rocking around mountain curves sent him again into sleep. When he woke he was in a room, moonlight falling in slats across the bed where Joanie slept beside him. Still he heard the sound of engines, a rhythmic pulse that assaulted the walls. He saw down an impossible tunnel the bathroom's nightlight, and closer the vague forms of furniture, a TV, hanging clothes. The sheets felt expensive; against them Joanie slept on her back, an arm flung out, hair fanned across the pillow. Her breath was deep and measured, an honest sleep that echoed the pulsing roar of invisible motion from the night beyond.

In that recurring dream came the cry: *DESTROY!* He sees the roadster crawl along the barren landscape, and some force moves his hands upward, the hammer falls. The car whimpers—it has been betrayed—and he swings again, and again. The cowl is barely creased, for the old metal has integrity. Then the door surrenders, a bit, and the line of captives cheer as the roadster moves ahead, limping into smoke. He hits the tail-light, which disintegrates, and a final blow catches the deck lid. The car moves stoically up the line, its stem mettle warding off blows, until it is overpowered by the weight of hammers.

Well, that's that, Mill says, watching it move off, to grow lower and lower. A part of his life is over.

Yep, the boy says. The last one. They're all gone now.

What did you say?

I heard the guards say the last Model A Ford was coming through tonight, and that was it. They ain't another left—anywhere.

Mill reels, struck by visions of the final buffalo sinking under the bullet's impact—whooping cranes, passenger pigeons, dodo birds. The sole survivor of a race dead—of old age or extermination. How much do we need? he wonders, recalling every time he had waxed that car's shiny flanks.

But the boy was right. Soon he does feel better. He has a sense of power, or revenge. With that hammer he can destroy. He can reduce an expensive new car to rubble in a few minutes, and this power warms him. Besides, he reasons, we need those parking places.

A sparkling convertible rolls into position; as the boy and Mill attack it, between swings Mill asks, *Are you sure they're employing?* For he will have to start his life over again, somewhere.

The next time he woke sunlight came through the louvered windows. Joanie was sitting in a chair, reading a magazine, a pile of butts in the ashtray at her elbow.

"Hey!" He fell back on the pillow, eyes tightly closed. Lights flashed, the bed rocked. The throbbing in his head was synchronized with that rhythmic pulse which moved beyond the room. When he put his hand on the throbbing he felt hair matted with dried blood. He remembered the bullet crashing through the window, the headlights, his body pitching forward.

"Hey! Where are we?"

"Hey yourself." She snubbed out her cigarette and walked to the doors, throwing them open. Beyond the small balcony, Mill could see the blue sky meeting an infinity of darker blue water. "Almost noon. I declare you're the dullest man I've ever spent a weekend with."

There was a wheeled tray between them, and from the copper pot which sat over a candle she poured him a cup of strong black coffee. Pain lapped his skull, and he took the cup with shaking hands. Emblazoned on the side was a blue and white crest, Cape Stevens Hotel.

"How're you this fine day?"

"Fine," he said, eyes tightly shut. His skull ached as if the bullet were lodged there; his eyes burned, his skin felt feverish. He was tired—for a week now he had not slept. "A little coffee, and I'll be just dandy."

"C'mon, get up and we'll see what the tide's washed in."

"How'd I get here?"

"I called the station yesterday," she said, "and a mental midget answered, honest to gawd, I couldn't understand a word."

Later she had been on her way to The Place, she said, and thought that she would check to see how every little thing was. She had found Mill lying in his own blood; he had obviously fallen against the window, cutting himself. "It's lucky I happened to stop, or you'd have been there all night."

"Why here?"

"You kept saying you had to get out of town." She lit another cigarette, the smoke jetting from her nose. "I did open your billfold to learn your name, Millard, just wanted to know who I was bringing here." He opened his eyes to see her smile.

In slow motion he dropped one leg, then the other to the floor, where his coveralls lay in a grey pile. Slowly he stood, and walked toward the bathroom; he stepped into the shower in dirty underwear, spun the huge chrome knobs, and heard no pipes rattle in these walls. Leaning against the wall he turned and saw in the mirror his reflection: sunken cheeks, dull eyes, stiff bloody hair, and then hot water flowed rusty red over him to blur the image.

When he emerged his arms and legs trembled. Hot water sent his heart pounding against ribs, and every beat was a throbbing pain that exploded in his head. He eased into the dirty imprint he had left on the bed, and pulled the covers over him as Joanie came from the balcony.

"Come on, let's get to the beach."

"I can't make it."

"Shoot, you'll feel fine, a little sun and salt air—"

"I can't move. Besides, I don't have any clothes."

"Sure you do." On the hanger she offered were slacks and a bright beach shirt. "These were Tony's, they ought to fit. And here's some shoes."

"I mean it, *reely*—"

"I'll help you." She threw back the covers and with a hand on each shoulder she levered him to a sitting position. One arm and then the other went into the shirt. "Let's leave three buttons undone," she said. "That's *racy.*" Then he was standing, and her fingers slid wet shorts down his trembling legs. She got on clean ones, snapping the elastic at his waist. Mill balanced his weight against her as the slacks were stepped into, drawn up. She buckled him, and walked his feet into sandals. Eyes still shut, he felt the comb pass through his hair, over the wound.

"Ought to have a couple stitches, I suppose," she said.

"Maybe we can find a doc in town."

He let her guide his elbow along the hallway and into the elevator. "We'll go around the lobby this time," she said, pushing B. The car stopped in a basement cluttered with suitcases, surfboards, boxes; she led him through this junk and up a short flight of metal stairs, to the door. The basement was oily-black, and when Mill stepped outside he was blinded by the fierce glare—the sand was a brilliant white that glazed off to the horizon's infinity of mirrors. Behind his shielded eyes the pain pounded like the surf.

On his arm Joanie hummed some melody. She led him toward the water, the cresting waves white on brilliant white. A terrific heat rose from the sand, and Mill felt his head spin; he focused on the patch of yellow a few inches ahead of his feet, and saw nothing—an area of tinfoil without definition. His heart pounded, skipped once, and he knew he was dying.

"Race you in," she said.

He sat on the sand and squeezed his eyes shut, his arms tight against his chest. His legs would not work, and he was blind.

"Hold this."

The light through one squinting eye was a knife, and looking up he saw Joanie undoing her clothes—black against the sun, her body edges glowing. She threw her dress in his lap. "And this." Something struck his leg as he swung the cloth over his head. Then she was kicking sand, strong legs striking the beach in little puffs.

Each sand grain glowed, a prism of refracted light. Even with the dress over his head the beach was a mirror, and under it the heat was intense. Heat waves swirled, mirages of dotted blue lines. His fingers sifted sand and came up with Joanie's sunglasses, which he put on. The pain did not recede but he could now define the beach, which Joanie raced across, from the surf, into which she splashed. A wave smashed into her, waist high, and she was swimming, head down, elbows up. He watched until she was a dot, and he became dizzy.

He went deeper under the dress, and the opening was like a distant tunnel. Eyes closed, he listened: the incessant roar of the surf, waves upon waves, the shrill alarm of gulls, his heartbeat, and—nothing. No sound of engines, radios, people. He rocked on the burning sand, sand trickling like time under his fingers. Sweat dripped from his forehead, down his bare arms—in this silent void he moved back, quit breathing, and entered a sleep that was almost mystical.

"Come on," Joanie said, tugging him to his feet. "Let's walk to Seaside."

She wore a bikini, two thin strips of bright cloth, and she shimmered in the golden heat. The brilliant floral design covered the lower third of her breasts, and he looked past to where the town wavered like a mirage. "I don't think I can make it."

"Sure you can" she said, pulling his arm. "It's not far, the heat distorts distance."

"No kidding, I can't."

One foot before the other, he concentrated on his legs. The sand sucked him back into his steps, and when he looked seaward he seemed to be skimming easily in reverse. Around him Joanie danced, dashing to the waves' edge, kicking— "Oh this water." She ran back, her skin powdered with golden beads. "Oh this beautiful sand." Under a thin layer of loose flesh there were plates of muscles—Mill noticed the high, rounded calves that stood out when she bounced on her toes, and the hard ridges across her back—muscles formed by her Daddy's love for competitive sports. "The sky—it's like ah ah a blue bowl!"

She danced while Mill slogged along, his feet impossible weights. When Joanie took the dress from his arm he looked up, and saw the littered beach: blankets were spread from surf to seawall in a confusion of color.

Joanie slipped the dress over her bikini, and they cut across the beach toward the Turnaround, through the odor of cocoa butter. A medicine ball flew past, was caught by a tall, bronzed boy who ran around them, laughing. Near the wall a rock group was shattering the air, and around the temporary bandstand danced a throng of half-naked kids.

In the crowd of tanned, muscular bodies Mill looked at his white, bleached arms, and then looked at the men who were looking at Joanie.

Up the stairs to the Turnaround, where a ceaseless, impatient line of cars circled the pylon designating the end of the Lewis and Clark Trail. Horns rattled against the shouts of college boys. Balloons rolled on the sea wind. Down the street, among the small shops, a Ferris wheel rotated toward the blazing sun.

Mill leaned against the seawall, legs trembling. He looked across the mass of sunbathers, stretching to the surf, the white-capped breakers, the ocean that spread to the shimmering horizon. At that line dividing sea and sky he saw a ship, a dark spot, which he focused on until all but that dot filled with darkness. The tunneled vision dizzied, and he hugged the wall's cement balustrade while the notes of the hard-rock band dotted the air.

"Be right back. Got to get some film."

He watched Joanie enter the shop, and when he turned he saw them: Eddie's gang.

They were grouped by the bandstand. Black leather jackets. Cycle caps tilted over foreheads. These clothes stood out against the bare, gyrating bodies of the beach dancers.

How had they followed him here to the land's end? He heard the sharp whine of the bullet, glass splintering—the headlights framing him for death. In the garage he imagined the roadster was now a total wreck, worked over with a ball-peen hammer.

Mill swallowed against the dryness, and a charge of fear left him shaking; the fingers that fitted the dime into the telescope trembled. The lens swung away from Sea Lion Rock, across the water, the beach, the wreckage of flesh on blankets, to the bandstand where sun blazed from a chrome guitar. In the shadow of the musicians stood the gang, black jackets, puchuko pants; they rocked to the guitar's anarchy, fingers snapping. Mill focused the telescope and scanned each pocked, narrow face, studied the gum chewing jaws.

They were all strangers.

"Ready?" Joanie took his arm, steered him along the crowded sidewalk. Young people from all over the state were in town for a crazy weekend, one of the last before school began; they walked easily in bathing suits, carrying guitars, beer, blankets. Tonight there would be a dance somewhere, and on the beach people would sleep around hundreds of driftwood fires.

"Wow, I'm hungry," Joanie said, fumbling in her pockets. "Give me two, and a Coke." The stand occupied five cubic feet, a niche in the line of small shops, and the owner reached out to hand Joanie the hot-dogs.

Five boys stumbled in a line, arms linked over shoulders, clearing the sidewalk. They wore college sweatshirts, carried quarts of beer, the lip barely visible from a paper sack. They slurred a song: *Ooooooohh the sun shines bright on Nellie Cartwright, she couldn't fart right–*. A few feet behind a city policeman followed apprehensively, his hand near his night-stick. Girls, crowded into an open convertible, yelled at the boys, who sang back: *her ass was aiiiiiir-tight.* Traffic was bumper to bumper, inching toward the Turnaround and back, in an endless, mindless circle.

Souvenir shops, taverns, a theater, the penny arcade, a salt-water taffy store, another which sold driftwood. These blurred in Mill's eye as he plodded beside Joanie, who walked rapidly, looking in each window, stopping to buy something to munch on. He waited in front of the bumper-cars while she went into a shop to buy a gift for a friend; the shop seemed to specialize in ashtrays made from clam shells, each with a painting of Sea Lion Rock. He watched the bumper-cars smashing together; heard the high, hysterical screams of girls, saw the grinning boys as they forced the little cars into impossible traffic jams. Electrical sparks fell from the ceiling runners, and the air was heavy with the smell of ozone. The noise filled his head, and his stomach tightened.

Joanie was beside him, holding up a clam shell ashtray, when shouts came from the beach; someone was talking through a bullhorn, the words unintelligible. They began walking again when Mill suddenly felt his lungs go empty– the street warped, the sidewalk rose and fell like a trampoline as Mill grabbed a parking meter.

"What's wrong?" Joanie asked.

The street tilted, inclined, the parking meter under his hands felt like rubber, falling away, springing back. There was a terrific roar in his ears, and he looked up to see a purple sedan rapping its exhaust pipes–he thought of Marty, as the sound lapped his mind in concentric waves.

"You know, I don't think I'll make it back."

The convertible full of girls inched in the opposite direction. Now the five drunk boys were sitting on top of the back seat, leaning over the trunk lid: *her ass was aiiiiirtight!*

The purple sedan rapped pipes beside the convertible, occupants leaning out to touch the girls' car. Mill saw mouths moving, felt the post falling from his hands. The noise and heat were overwhelming; his breath came short, the tic clawed at his face. Panic, the fear of dying on a public street, overwhelmed him, but he was too weak to move.

"Hey, I think I'm gonna pass out."

"What?" Joanie's hand was cupped to her ear, her expression a question mark. "What'd you say?"

"I think I'm–"

Now one of the boys stood on the convertible's trunk lid, and swinging a quart beer bottle by the neck he threw it overhand at the purple sedan. The windshield shattered; a shower of glass rose into the air and hung suspended like a curtain of diamonds. Light spun from the prisms, shifting as each crystal turned slowly, and even before the fragments fell two cops ran past. The next boy missed the sedan–his bottle arced across the sidewalk, spinning slowly to crash into the plate glass window of the driftwood shop.

The last thing Mill saw was a squad of National Guard sprinting through traffic, their clubs at port arms. Another bottle spun across the sun, and as Mill sat on the sidewalk his eyes rolling up into his head, toward the ceaseless pain that throbbed in his skull like a small engine, he heard, somewhere, the bottle shatter into a million fragments.

–Come on, Joanie said, tugging him to his feet. Golden light diffused through his squinting eye, and she stood over him, black against the sun, her body edges glowing. She wore a bikini, two thin strips of bright cloth that covered the lower third of her breasts. Her navel held an emerald and each facet glowed, a prism of refracted light –Let's walk to California.

–I don't think I can make it, he said.

–It's not far, she said. –The heat distorts distances.

He threw the dress from his head and began to rise.

Under his hands the beach was incredibly hot, and he noticed that the entire area, for as far as he could see, had been paved flat and the asphalt painted a sandy-yellow. But as he followed her he seemed to drift across the pavement, feet moving easily. His head felt light, as if glowing under a halo, and when he looked up he saw blue sky beyond the traumatized skull; like a roof with a hole in it.

–Oh, this pavement, Joanie said, skipping on the hot asphalt.–It's like, wow! Her heavy golden breasts rolled with her shoulders; her thighs stretched against the tiny cloth. The emerald in her navel projected light scenes like a thousand miniature TV sets.

–Hey! I was just kidding about the walk, she said. She opened the convertible's door for him, and danced around the car, her hair rising and falling like slow subterranean movements: –Here, hold this, she said, throwing her dress into his lap. –Keep the glasses.

Mill leaned back in the hot upholstery, noticing how her breasts plunged downward to almost touch the steering wheel's rim. The emerald in her navel glowed, and as Mill leaned forward to take a closer look he saw in each prism a projected vignette: the two of them in bed, on the beach, swinging southward in the big convertible into the Redwood National Forest. He leaned back into the hot leather–this was where he belonged, this was his Place. If they followed the yellow eight-lane beach south they would, he knew, be in California by tomorrow lunchtime.

–I really am in love with you, Millard, Joanie said.

Her long, fleshy leg tapered to the gas pedal, which she held to the floor. The wheel spun effortlessly in her strong hands as she swung the car to avoid a high wave, or a low gull, her blonde hair streamed over golden shoulders, stretching to the back seat.

—You see, it was love at first sight, because you do remind me of my brother, she said, looking at him from hooded eyes.—I love you and I'm going to see that you get the best doc in California. He'll patch up the hole in your head, and at the same time we'll have that tic removed.

—Sounds great, Mill said, pulling the dress over his head to shut out the wind that whistled across it like a flute.

Beyond the blue horizon—

Through open doors an ocean wind cooled Mill's face and the sheets wet with sweat. He opened burning eyes to a dark room and, beyond the balcony, the night. From somewhere came the local radio station's theme song: *a new day's already begun, Beyond the blue horizon lies the setting sun—*. The clock's luminous face said 12:30. On the food tray he saw her note: *Back soon.*

He had not eaten for almost two days, but the cold dinner on the tray turned his stomach. He poured a glass of wine and laid down again to ease the ache in his kidneys. Drifting inland came the sound of singing, and from somewhere in the hotel he heard laughter. From Seaside, the high wail of a siren.

In the nightstand's drawer he found cigarettes and the TV's remote control device. He lit a cigarette, gagged on the thick smoke, and snubbed it out as the dot of light popped into the dark. A hum, it sprang larger, and the light grew square. Figures swirled into the screen, began talking: *Vegcutter, cuts whole chunks of meat, cheese, makes dozens of tomato slices in just minutes, hundreds of onion slices, thousands of french-fried potatoes—*Mill's stomach rolled as the pile of chopped food grew: *how much do we need?*

"And now it's time for the Saturday night Late Show. Tonight's fine feature is *The General Died At Dawn,* starring Gary Cooper, Madeleine Carroll, and Akim Tamiroff–"

Mountain ringed with stars. Heavy block printing; strong contrasts–quivery music. Shot of the person when introduced: Cooper, smooth-faced. Madeleine resembled Garbo. 1930: a train crossing China, bandits ahead. Cross-section of the times: US Army officer, showgirl, traveling salesman, missionary, British colonialist, educated Jap. Intrigue. The Orient. "Haven't I seen you somewhere?" asks the missionary. "Hong Kong? Singapore? Shanghai?" "What's a nice girl like you doing on a train like this?" Madeleine smiles.

Train stopped. Bandits, or rebels, capture a Chinese general. Cooper dealing cleverly with these stumbling Orientals; they're no match for his inscrutable Western mind.

Jeezus, whatever happened to Akim Tamiroff? Killed in WW II? or maybe still in Hollywood, selling used cars, tract houses?

Did my parents see this, I wonder: captured, thrilled, dazed by the verisimilitude of screen and sound; audience stumbling sleepily on popcorn into the street empty of traffic. Climb up into their car–from curb to running board to floor to seat–into the pure smells of enamel and leather. Ride slowly toward home, where an ice box thrives on ice.

Saw that last February? March? After a long day in the library browsing through *Liberty,* circa '39-43. Good war covers: Hitler as a jackass, Mussolini a buzzard, Tojo a spider in his bloody web. A simple view of global war: why, they're just axis animals, and a little DDT

Click the channel changer and the screen blinks three times: man pulls to curb in a '35 Ford roadster; white sidewalls, top down. Jumps out and into a phone booth: "Listen Chief, have I got a Scoop. Hold the Presses! You remember that guy who went to the hot seat?"

44th floor. Ape hovers in background.

Flip channels.
Sedan rips around city corner, spins, hits some citizens. Roadster veers, spins. Cut to George Raft telling Ray Milland: "We got to frame that lousy politician, see. We start a rumor, feed it to the papers. See?"

Eddy Arnold's photo on the front page, under headline: LINKED TO

will knock out Tojo. Good war for my father, only time in his life he's made any money. Presidential E for Effort—and a husky paycheck.

Wow, what wheels—the streets so wide, empty, great. Let's see, "Monster and the Girl," I think, ca. 1939. Ellen Drew, Robert Paige, Rod Cameron in a walk-on. Yeah, guy's unjustly executed, has brain transferred to an ape goes after those who framed him. Pale parody of King Kong, but good. Science will save us. Journalists will inform us. *Stop the presses—a scoop!* Yeah, I'll drink to that.

Great. Pierce-Arrow, by the headlights. Spare tires. Window shade. Spotlight through windshield.

If art mirrors the times, what were people thinking about? Simple conflicts, in black and white: gangsters trying to corrupt the incorruptible politician. But the simplicity of the crimes, of the people who believe flimsy rumors,

FATAL CRASH. People on sidewalk: "Didja read this?" "I don't believe it." "I do."

"Gimme a gun."

Flip channels. Street scene. Shouting. Papers waved, with headline: LOCAL MAN MURDERED. Susan Hayward pulls up in a 1940 Plymouth coupe. "What happened?" "Brekker boy killed Poppy, the colored man who's watched over him for 25 years. Up in that old house." "Let's get him," one cries. "Lynch him." "Yaar." They move down the main street, with baseball bats.

"Lock up your daughters. He's a loony."

"I'm gonna get me that reward the paper's offerin."

The loony in a shabby room, tells Susan Hayward: "I just wanted to come back to life. To be among people." He gives her a silk dress, which she exclaims over: "Gee whillikers."

spoken or published—the whole world seemed four blocks long.

And the simplicity of the solution, too, which depended on direct action.

Ah yes, *Among the Living,* Albert Dekker, Harry Carey, France Farmer, Archie Twitchell—whatever happened to Archie Twitchell?

Forget that simple war blooming on the horizon, the big news is a dead Negro in a deserted house—not because he died, but because they might be next, and a good lynching is something to do. Tunnel vision. Could a whole town get excited about a killing, or the papers give it headlines?

Me too.

Last time I saw this I was hiding in my own

Flips channels.

Bare room. Bunch of old drunks in stark setting. Charles Bickford introducing Greta Garbo: "This here's my daughter, Anna Christy."

Flips channels.

Man and wife walking on a quiet street. Car races past. Whiskey bottle thrown, hits and kills their child. Broken glass. Mother hysterical. Punks laugh. Exhaust roar fades. Father shaking fist.

shabby room pull the covers over. But things just aren't that simple and perhaps never were. My father, walking the streets for any kind of work; my mother terrorized by their poverty.

Fuzzy picture. Awfully old, or this is a Frisco channel. Stagey. Theatrical gestures. Long silences. Hard to imagine what kind of audience this played to. Granny, perhaps.

Oh christ — Keefe Brasselle (and whatever happened to him?) in Chicago, mad at the world, one-man vendetta to get those kids. Speech on law and order by Frank Lovejoy, who's a cop when he isn't posing as a commie for the FBI.

Flips channels.

Gary Cooper slugs a Chinese officer,
leaps the balcony, grabs the girl,
heads for the train.

Men chasing an ape with a human brain; guns flash.

Reporter has his pad and pencil out—Scoop.

Politician moves in on George Raft: "Okay, you crook, now you're going to get what's coming to you. I vowed—"

Albert Dekker with brain size of an ape's is moving across lawn of deserted house, a bullet in him; guns flash, a simple expression of surprise and pleasure crosses his face. "I just wanted to be... among... people."

Charles Bickford embracing Greta Garbo and some old lady in a wide hat—they're all drunk, crying, in stark room. Long, long silence.

"Okay you punk," says Keefe Brasselle. "Now you're going to get what's coming to you. I vowed to clean the streets—"

The sound tracks merge their music into one continuous climactic overture, rising together in harmony as good in its various forms stamps out evil, and one by one the stations sign off—

goodnight   goodnight   goodnight
beyond the blue horizon
goodnight

As if in a dream he felt hot hands against his chest. When he opened his eyes he saw only the TV's dot patterns bouncing against the darkness; then he saw her silhouetted against the moonlight that filtered through the louvered doors. She hunched over him, her hands gently rubbing across his stomach, her hair falling against his legs.

He closed his burning eyes as her hands slid his shorts down. Slowly her strong fingers pushed through pubic hair and closed. He gasped, throat locked against the thrill. Her hair fell over his hot, feverish skin like a whip, and her lips touched his navel, nibbled lightly around his groin. When her wide mouth closed tightly around him he stiffened—hot *damn am I dreaming?*

She released him, sucking in breath, and he opened his eyes. In the dark room he could see the high curve of her shoulders, the fall of her breasts, the outline of whiteness where her bikini had covered them. She threw back the covers, her moan a lonesome song as she raised up from the bed, and swung a long leg over him.

She was on her knees, then sitting, her haunches spread, a leg on each side of him. He felt her hand guide him upward, felt the tissue open. *Oh oh oh*—she began to rotate her body, grinding him under those wide, tanned hips. His impulse was to reach out, to hold her, but his arms would not respond; he lay quietly, peacefully, under her moving body, feeling her fingers tear at his stomach.

Faster she moved, crying *oh oh oh* until he felt her stiffen, the plates of muscles contract, and she fell forward, her breasts spreading across his chest—*ohhhhhhh gawdamn!*

Perhaps he fell asleep—for a minute, an hour—but when he again opened his eyes she was still awake, her weight against him. Her face lay in the hollow between his neck and shoulder, and her fingers gently massaged his forehead. When she finally spoke it was a whisper very near his ear. "Who's Arma?"

The voice came like a dream from the pillow. He was suddenly aware of people singing along the beach, the shouts of college boys, and when the moment passed he dropped to another level; here everything was soft, cloud-like, in the fuzziness of fever. "Who?" he might have said.

"Arma Geddon. You were talking in your sleep." She moved hard wide hips against his groin, as if coaxing him to open up. "Want to tell Joanie the whole story?"

"No," he said, burning eyes closed, his mind dropping like an elevator level by level—the paved beach, parking lots, cities that contained their traffic, wide empty streets, parking places, no parking meters, a gas station on one comer instead of four, dirt roads, alleys, small towns, open fields.

"No," he thought he said, "I don't want to tell Joanie. Joanie wouldn't understand. Mill doesn't understand. Arma Geddon," he thought he said, laughing into her fanning hair, still damp with the odor of salt water, "Arma I haven't met yet, but she'll come, you can bet. Even Joanie will know her.

"But Joanie couldn't understand the rest—because she's never been poor. Can you imagine my family out scrabbling in the yard, picking up pieces of my diploma, taping the parts together to insure some kind of future—in the same way that my mother saves old bottles of medicine. As if that diploma existed."

"What do you mean-mean-mean?"

"They think I graduated—but *I quit.*"

His mind rolled with the tide, the night, lapping memories; he thought he was talking but the motion of speech was his teeth chattering. This was like death: on an inevitable night, the death-bed, the final words forced through feverish teeth, the confession. From down a long tunnel Joanie's voice echoed: "So what-what-what? What does it matter-matter-matter? A degree's not important-important-important."

"To a family like mine it is—you've got to be poor to know."

He knew it was useless to tell her *why* he had quit college, yet he was telling, because he hadn't told it to anyone else or possibly, he realized later, possibly he wasn't telling her, possibly he was talking gibberish, words confused by fever, or possibly he was dreaming that he was talking, that she was pressing her cool hands against his face, urging him to talk. He thought he was telling her about college:

You have to understand how I felt—for almost five years I worked my ass off, studying day and night, learning, surviving, keeping alive—

because I was *afraid* of failing. I was afraid

of lousy 8 to 5 jobs, work clothes, mortgage, kids, bitter wife. That's the vision that sent me to college—and I was making it. He thought he was telling about the campus in September, leaves scattered across the quad by a chilly wind—

and into it steps

a thin excited boy with one work suit,

a modest scholarship, yearning for knowledge.

Around him drifted tanned young men, Harris Tweeds, pipes, smiling coeds on their arms. Chimes rang from the tower. The scene was from an old movie, and he looked around the halls of ivy for Ronald Coleman.

I knew I didn't belong–it was a mistake.

But dammit I'd come too far, across a continent, and I worked to stay. I didn't dare fail fail fail–family, future depended on my success. And I did well: grades, but more that that I tested myself, and discovered that I *enjoyed* learning things, which is *real* learning.

And that's the way it went for almost five years:

Study study gawdamn study; work during vacations; work part-time during school; broke all the time.

But enjoying it, you understand: the more I got into architecture the more obsessed I became about *building things–building things,*

the use of space, materials; the vision of structures rising smoothly and magnificently into the sky.

I felt I was getting somewhere. I thought about all that money waiting–I'd never had any–but more it was doing a job you loved.

Building things, and doing them well.

Then the bottom fell out, sometime in that final year.

I'd studied the history of architecture, knew all the magnificent structures:

Propylaea, Temple of Jupiter, Stoa of Attalus,

Odeon of Herodes Atticus;

that masterpiece of Byzantine architecture,

the Church of Saint Sophia–even felt I knew

personally Anthemius and Isidorus.

The Church of San Lorenzo, Baptistery of St. John,

Giotto's Campanile.

The Sphinx of King Chephren, the Pyramids of Giza.

Evan's reconstructions at Knossos, Schlieman's excavations at Mycenae.

The Cathedrals at Amiens, Rouen, the Notre Dame de Paris.

The Roman Forum, the Arch of Constantine, St. Peter's Basilica, the Colosseum, Pantheon.

The works of Christopher Wren.

Wright's Taliesin West, Husser House, Imperial Hotel, Second Jacobs House.

I'd done a detailed plan of the Pyramid of King Zoser.

I'd built scale models of the Parthenon, Chartres Cathedral, the Kaufmann House.

I loved the materials, the technical terms, loved the words:

Doric, Ionian—don't they *sound* like their shapes?—

vaulted arches, flying buttresses, stained glass, rose windows.

Slowly

I began to realize what I should have known:

in theory we were prepared to build the Parthenon;

in practice we'd be drawing plans for tract houses—

costly houses, perhaps, but Jerry-built shacks.

Then I began to look around me—development projects, shabby boxes, tenements, slums and brand-new slums.

Architects, city-planners—what a lousy job we'd done.

What a lousy use of space and materials and knowledge.

What I saw depressed the hell out of me: poor design, no planning, shoddy work. We'd failed the people.

Thence cometh the Grand Irony—

the Grand Irony was that while we'd been studying the great historical examples of architecture—

structures that have lasted

hundreds, in some cases thousands, of years—

we were planning houses which were intended *not* to last.

Throw 'em up, tack 'em together, tear 'em down.

Shoddy workmanship is celebrated;

craftsmanship, a sense of caring, is a vice.

Then the dream started:

first it was houses, and in the dream

pre-fabricated duplicates of the Parthenon were thrown together and immediately bulldozed down. The government subsidized this.

Later the dream concerned cars—how much do we want?

Detroit's endless rapid assembly line.

Think about it: rather than repair good shoes we toss them away; we drive a car two years and it's ready for scrap.

The backseat of that car would last a Red Chinese 500 years.

We work hard to wear things out.

Planned obsolescence. Nothing should last.

Whatever happened to the American pioneer spirit— make do with what you have. Yankee ingenuity.

Build it well, fix it when it breaks. Quality, not quantity.

How much do we need?

Anyway, I think I'm telling you that I quit

classes, studying. I began to have other dreams,

crazy dreams of the whole nation paved over, asphalt and concrete from ocean to ocean. Parking lots big as states.

Shopping centers the size of cities.

One morning I awoke and looked in the mirror,

saw something had happened   to my face—this tic

this tic—the cheek muscle kept jerking.

After that it was all downhill.

To avoid dreaming I didn't sleep, began to watch TV,

oh, I caught every late-late show, channel by channel.

At first they just kept me from sleep, then I began to watch,

and finally, slowly, like thread pulled through a needle

I began regressing *into* them:

I loved their simple conflicts. Hell with the plot,

I watched for the *tone* of the times, the *moods*.

Thinking how simple, beautiful things were: open places,

fields, solid houses, cars designed simply to last twenty years

and they did.

I went back in time, spent days in the library,

reading old magazines and newspapers. I reconstructed the

Past in my head.
Take 1948, for example: what was it like?
Quiet, in that interim between World War II and Korea.
Veterans in college; starting small businesses;
trying to find a home they could buy;
waiting for a new car, driving a dependable Model A.
There were small stores that showed a profit.
There were people who repaired shoes, and did it well.
There was a nice balance between gas stations and cars.
There were plenty of parking places, without meters.
There were kids with crew-cuts or long black hair
swept to a duck's ass, who hung out at Gilmore stations
but were not hoods. There were clear skies, green grass,
and Business still showed a profit.
People listened seriously to the radio.
Entering into that Past that I knew was good,
I came back: back to simple streets, to quiet things.
Thinking about craftsmanship and how we've lost it,
I naturally began to recall my roadster. I'd built it
with my own hands, several times. That's craft,
caring, loving your work.
I thought about Fronty, a real craftsman, who could
never do sloppy work. You can't find people like him
anymore,
and that's a national disaster.
That's why I came back.
But you can't understand what I mean.

Chapter 9

"Why don't we?" Mill asked. He felt great: the sun was a giant pump, sending heat and energy into his back.

"Why don't we what?" Joanie's voice floated lazily on the sea breeze. Her head rested on her arms, and the tension of flesh had pulled the breast on this side free of the bikini. Already the soft white skin was beginning to burn.

"Why don't we do it?" Mill asked. .

"You mean here?" Joanie said, laughing. "On the beach?"

"I mean why not go to California?" he said.

He moved toward her and felt a glowing surface pain along every body crease–he was getting burned, and the beach was like sandpaper. Yet, as he floated on the blanket, beneath that golden motor that pumped heat and energy into him, he felt great.

He had been the first person on the beach this morning.

Awake at dawn, he had showered, dressed and hurried to the dining room with a terrific hunger. He ordered a large breakfast, ate quickly, and signed their room number to the bill.

The fever had passed, his head was calm, and he felt good. Sitting in the sun with a second cup of coffee, the golden horizon stretching endlessly before him, he knew that there had been no shot–he had simply stumbled because of fatigue, and had fallen against the window, breaking it. There was no danger; *he would not die* in the absurd violence of Loaner's Corner. Nor, after last night, did he feel any responsibility toward the Past.

"Well..." he said. "Why don't we go to California?"

"Ummmm. I had been thinking of Majorca. Or Hydra. Y'know?"

He had been thinking of San Francisco, someplace accessible, and he slid across the space to her blanket, the sand scraping his tender flesh. His hand crossed her back, over the hundreds of sweat drops that blossomed into the sun. Fingers traced down the vertebrae one by one, to the place where the skin became a cleft. Joanie sighed, turned lazily toward him. "We could go," he said, thinking of wide, palm-lined streets, washed in California sun.

He was not prepared for what she did: raising slightly, she kissed him. The brush of lips was quick; he barely sensed her hair against his shoulder, tasted the salt on her wide upper lip, when she lay back down—but the moment hovered like a mirage before his tinted gaze: her eyes half-closed, her tongue a delicate pink tip. Never before had he seen such a *mature,* sensual expression as in that flickering, almost casual moment.

"We could go—" he said, "back to the room."

She lowered the sunglasses from her hair to the bridge of her nose. "Sure. It's lunch time."

Mill stood, almost aware of the blanket under his arm that cut like barbed wire; across the golden sand they walked, his body glowing with a visible radiance. Ahead the hotel blossomed with activity: all chairs along the seawall were filled, the antique sunbathers watching the long-legged woman and the thin man walk toward them. Mill was only aware of the flesh beside him that rolled with every step above the bikini's elastic, and that handful that sleeked from thigh into buttock.

They walked past the heads that stared after them, into the lobby's darkness.

"Good morning, Mr. Maloney, Mrs. Maloney," said the man. "We hope that you're enjoying your stay."

Bare heels slapped the tile floor. The lobby was dark and cool, and in the elevator that whisked them smoothly to the third floor Mill slipped his hand around Joanie's waist.

"Lord," she said. "I'm hungry."

In the room a seaward breeze sucked the door shut, and as the curtains near the open window lowered, Mill leaned against the lock's button. He watched Joanie stoop to pick something up, saw her buttocks spread and swell into roundness, the leg muscles tighten as she stood. A small roll of flesh bulged at each hip, riding above the suit's elastic. Her back was full, the ribs like templates. Even the backs of her arms he found sexy.

"This yours?" He took the paper, a creased and greasy napkin with a rough sketch of the Sports Special. It must have fallen from his coveralls.

"Whoooee," she said, shaking her hair out. "I need a shower."

Mill stepped forward, taking her elbow. The skin under his fingers whitened as he pressured her around to face him. He saw her surprise fade, eyelids soften, lips open, a trace of soft pink tongue swell along her lower teeth. She leaned under his pressure, her mouth brushing his, stopping for a second against his lips and he tasted the thin aroma of tobacco, chlorophyll gum, green mouthwash. He sensed her body lightly against his burning flesh; against his crotch the plate of her hip side hovered.

As their lips threatened to separate Mill grabbed her hair. He pressed into her his lips, his body, and she did not resist.

Nor did she respond. He moved closer, moving into her dead weight. When he broke the kiss she opened her eyes, brushed her hair back. "Hey, a shower, okay?" she said.

One hand still held her hair, and the fingers of the other moved a few inches upward, mid-back. The bow gave, the suit's top fell away under the weight of breasts. That hand came forward, cupping the warm elongated flesh that almost fit the fingers. Mill stroked the breast, from the incline's start near the clavicle to the nipple, large and dark.

He traced this outline, and when he looked up he saw that her expression had not changed—the lips barely parted, the eyes neutral. He kissed her, receiving only the edges of her lips.

But this passive, submissive reaction excited him more than if she had suddenly begun to strip. His hand closed tightly on her naked breast and his tongue forced itself into her mouth. Against her his hips began to move, and then he was walking backwards, his hands against her buttocks, drawing her toward the bed.

He buried his face between her breasts, his hands searching across her throat, the wide shoulders, the nipples near his ears. Between his hands her waist narrowed, and the stomach muscles tensed. Her skin was firm, soft, golden brown, and the muscles were hard beneath his searching fingers. Down they went across the widening thighs, hard calves.

He sat on the edge of the bed, staring at the triangle of cloth – bright green and red, the colors danced before his eyes. He looked to her face, a foreshortened perspective past the white breasts, dark nipples; she had her head turned slightly, eyes half-shut, as if squinting to inspect something far out to sea.

His hand passed over the cloth and with shaking fingers he undid the ties. The cloth fell away to reveal a white triangle of skin, dark matted hair; he buried his face there, arms linked around her legs, and as he bit her he fell backwards, pulling her over him.

"What the hell—" But he held fast, moving against her pelvis, taking her full weight, trying in his excitement to get all his body in her. She rolled across the bed, dragging him, his teeth biting her thighs, belly, the dark hair. He tasted cocoa-butter, baby oil, the fine grains of sand.

Her legs pushed him back, driving him from the bed, and then he realized she was shouting: "That *hurts,* dammit!"

"Listen," he said, not expecting this resistance. "Listen, it can be beautiful. Really *beautiful*—you know that word?" He crawled back onto the bed, where her long, long legs tapered from toes to the cage of her hips. He thought he knew now what might have caused the riot at Seaside yesterday—or at least knew how men could be driven to the pitch of madness by the sight of so much bare flesh.

"Listen," he said, "if you don't want to, say so."

"I only said it hurts." She laughed, and laid her strong hand over his, palm down, the fingers interlacing. Her other hand stroked her own thigh, slowly caressing the skin.

"Don't you like sex?"

"Lots," she said, laughing. "I have an erotic orientation."

Although he wasn't quite sure what she meant, the admission sent a wave of emotion along his skin. He moved against the cool sheet, studying her breasts, tummy, the dark chiaroscuro. Her fingers tightened on his wrist, pulling him to her.

He rolled against her, his hand stroking the skin over her ribs. A cool breeze came through the window from far out at sea, and he shivered. Her fingers traced the bones of his chest, trickling like sand across his stomach and then she was half sitting, tugging at the elastic of his trunks. He closed his eyes and felt her hands slide along his hips, her fingers close around him. He shivered as her thumb and forefinger worked in a slight, thrilling motion; when she dropped her head he could not breathe.

Her lips tightened until he could feel every ridge. Then something raised his back, arching it higher, and as she pulled away his hand touched her breast—he spun to one side, hands reaching empty air, back taut, and suddenly, caught in the emptiness of mid-air, he felt himself come: *ohhh no!* he said, surprised, seeing in a flash the ceiling, her smiling face, the infinity of blue beyond the window. Uncontrollably his hips jerked, violent motions like a dog hung up.

"Gawdamn," Joanie said, laughing, head thrown back. "Gawdamn gawdamn."

Mill closed his eyes, heard that distant engine of the surf pounding outside, and near his ear heard Joanie's quick breathing. Her hand slid across his stomach, and for the first time he was aware of his sunburn—her fingers were like ice against his fiery flesh. Her fingers coolly held him, thumb teasing the tip. "Relax," she said.

He opened one eye. The veins in her breasts were large and blue, the nipples dark and swollen. Her hip moved against his, her hand dropped to the hollow beneath his testicles, where the giant ache throbbed. She touched, and he felt the sac shrivel with pleasure.

Then she took his hand and placed it against her stomach, where there was a hard central muscle exactly the size of his palm. She slid the fingers downward, through matted hair, guiding its motion. "Do that," she said. He felt the skin divide, slide back, open to a smaller crease. Her wide hips began to rock against the finger's pressure. "A little faster," she said, her voice a whisper. "Good. That's good." Her head was thrown back over the pillow, eyes closed. His other hand took her breast, closed on it; the nipple began to swell under his fingers and he shifted his head until he could touch the nipple with his tongue.

"Ohhhh," she said, and as her hips tightened on his hand she frightened him: *ohhh,* she said, only it was a sharp bark, a yelp, which grew louder until the fourth time her cry rang in his head, a sharp piercing cry of agony and pleasure. *Yes. Oh* (breath) *oh* (breath) *quick–*

When he rolled over he was surprised that he had anything to insert, but her fingers guided him large and hard into the blackness. As he penetrated her he felt waves of emotion, inch by inch, and finally it was as though three fingers had closed on him.

Her hips shuddered, came to meet him, fell away; her fingers raked his back, teeth bit into his shoulder. "I'm fine," she said. "But keep going."

He reached down and wrapped his arms around her legs, tilting her toward his stroke. Their bodies adhered with the sweat that rolled from skin, broke with a sucking noise; he drove himself into her, the suntan oil lubricating motion.

Eyes closed, he thought of her breasts, her lips, the swing of long legs–recalled that first time she had driven into Fronty's; that night when they had gone to The Place–he had never imagined that they would someday be together in the luxury of this bed, her legs spread for him. The thought of the *possibility* coiled down his spine; into his nuts, and gathered intensity.

"Can I leave it in?"

"Yes, but—"

As he came her legs tightened around his waist, squeezing. Then they lay quietly together, slowly coming down. Her fingers stroked his back, and he felt himself shrivel within her. Then he got up, surprised once again at the size of her breasts, and took her hand. "C'mon." He led her into the bathroom, where he saw in the mirror the brick-red color his body had assumed. Turning on the shower, he pulled her in. The cold water cut him like little knives, cutting away burned flesh, sweat, sand, oil. He worked the soap between his hands and when he had a good lather he shifted it to her golden flesh, hands sliding across her wide breasts and working downward.

Later he would remember with intensity only the details: the wide nipples, flecked with a lighter pigment; the soft tissue around her inner thigh; the hard central muscle of her stomach, sitting just below the flesh; the soft invisible pubic hairs at the beltline, which spread wide and dark below; the way she knowingly used her fingers, thrilling him with the least touch; the lines that lightly segmented her lips; the odor of *skin* she kept after that shower.

His hands slid across her wide back, the lather spinning away under the water's pressure. Her waist was a beautiful slow contour, merging into buttocks. Suddenly he pressed himself against her and she opened, hands locked on the faucets for support; he guided himself into her from behind, his hands reaching around front to keep it in, and as she bent further, head down, he slid both hands upward, to grasp the sleek, lather-slick breasts. He forgot about the garage, the Sports Special—that slim dream—Loaner's Corners, Tonto, Eddie and her gang, whatever obligation he thought he had to his family; he forgot about all that which he would have to return to tomorrow.

The towel was like ground glass against his sunburned body—in the mirror he glowed, an angry red reflection. It was no longer possible to distinguish the work lines at his neck and wrists, where grease had recently ridden like a disease. He carefully dried himself, humming snatches of the local theme song—*beyond the blue horizon, a new day's already begun* and when he stepped into the room he heard Joanie on the phone: "Send up enough for two *hungry* people—oh and a bottle of red wine." She wore a white terry cloth beach robe that was very short and open at the front; as she hung up the phone and turned to encircle him with her arms, he saw that she wore nothing under it.

"I've ordered lunch for us," she said. "Why, there's no reason to go out!" She kissed him with her lower lip, sliding it between his teeth. "I also told the man we intend to keep these rooms until Tuesday."

Chapter 10

In the hot noon sun the station slept, lulled by the humming insects of the fields. Near the road the metal Hudson-Terraplane sign hung on rusty hinges, and a car passed with the slap-slap-slap of tires against hot pavement. Otherwise, he heard only the mild hum of the air conditioning unit.

"It's been real," Joanie said, smiling. "See you around."

"How about tomorrow night?" Mill studied her tan skin that spread against the rich leather; she wore only the bright bikini, and Mill thought she had never looked so beautiful.

He sat in coveralls, reluctant to open the door and enter the intense heat. Under his arms the sharp cloth cut into his sunburn, and he knew he would soon be miserable.

"Uhmmmm–I might be gone. If I'm in town I'll call."

"Gone," he said, "Where?"

"Mallorca," she said, laughing. "Hydra. Acapulco. Who knows?"

"Okay," he said, not understanding. He opened the door and a cloud of dry heat rolled in. "Tomorrow, you give me a call–if you're in town. And hey: *thanks for everything.*"

He slammed the door and Joanie swung the twenty-foot convertible across the gravel and onto the highway, waving once. Mill stood in freshly laundered coveralls, listening to the noise of the insects that churned the fields, and the angry scream of a chainsaw high on Mt. Scott. The convertible approached The Curve and disappeared in the mirage of heat waves.

Beside the garage sat the Alpha, falling to rust, two of its tires missing. In the lube room was the roadster, and Mill noted with great relief that its paint was smooth and untouched.

"Where in holy hell you been?" Fronty rolled his chair from the office, then spun it sideways.

A square of plywood covered the shattered pane, and Mill stepped closer to see what had actually happened here. "Somebody try to break in?"

"Hell, that's a bullet hole. Bullet's stuck in the cash register. And somebody stole the tires and Weber carbs offn the sports car."

Mill shoved his hands deep into his pockets and felt the cloth cut into his shoulders. He kicked at the gravel, and went into the lube room, where it was twenty degrees cooler. He walked around the roadster, his hand touching its lacquer slick sides.

"Where the hell you been anyway?" Fronty asked, propelling his chair across the gravel into the lube room. "Your parents called, some other guy's been calling for you. I didn't know what to tell them—"

"I took a couple days off, okay?" Mill tugged at the collar that cut his skin. The sunburn was beginning to diminish, and if he didn't peel too badly he would have a good tan.

"You in some kind of trouble?" Fronty squinted through the oily darkness of the room, searching for an answer.

"No, no trouble."

A truck rolled to the pumps and Mill was outside, the sun laid on his back like a whip. "Yessir?"

"Three gallons." The farmer's face was beet-red, dripping sweat, and strained with inherent suspicion. "That's regular, now."

Mill moved around the truck, inserted the nozzle and waited, standing in the sharp smells of gasoline and the old hay and alfalfa. Suddenly he knew he could not stay here tomorrow, or the next day, he would begin to look for another job. Not to please his father, but to save his own sanity.

He hung up the nozzle and went to get the bills, which were creased and grimy. The farmer finally let go of them, and, possibly smiling, he said: "Yer open."

"Open every day, except on the Sabbath."

"I mean yer open. In front."

135

Mill looked down and saw that the lower buttons on his coveralls, opened by Joanie, were still undone.

The wheel lifted them shakily upward, into the cool night air. Lights played against the backsides of leaves, yellow and iridescent, and then they were lifted above the tree tops, into the darkness that stretched away into infinity. As the wheel reached its apex they heard only the trembling machinery that sent its sound vibrating up the struts from the ancient central sprocket. At the top the cool night air carried the smell of lilac and wisteria, and from their left the dark smells of the Willamette.

"See there!" Joanie shouted, pointing across the river toward town. "Up there, that's my house!"

"Oh come on," Mill laughed, "you can't possibly see–"

"I can! I left the light on so I could."

The wheel began to rotate them downward, and as the car above blotted out their view Mill grinned and squeezed her hand. She was like a child, her lap filled with kewpie dolls and teddy bears and plaster statues of dogs. It was Ladies' Nite at Oaks Park, and everything cost a dime. She had won her trophies on the ring toss and the rifle range and the baseball throw and bingo–she had won, on every game of chance. Her father had instilled in her this sense of competition: *it's not how you play the game, dammit–it's winning.* Mill thought of that game room, filled with trophies.

Warm air rose to meet them; they descended into the glare of the midway, into the noise of organ music from the roller rink. The Ferris wheel shuddered, groaned, bucked, and Joanie took his hand, pressing it tightly.

Under the oak trees cars were parked at all angles, and Mill could hear the shouts of kids stealing hubcaps, or the laughter of the rink rats who now sat in backseats, drinking. They stumbled back and forth as if on skates, clutching at their tight-sweatered girls, urging them into a car where the radio pounded out the notes of violence. Mill was reminded of Eddie and her gang, and realized he had hardly thought of them since last Friday when the bullet had crashed past his head. There hadn't been any more anonymous calls. Today, when the phone rang it was Joanie—she was still in town, and if he wanted to do something—

The wheel swung them upward into darkness, into the cool night air, and the town unfolded toward the shifting horizon. At the top, the wheel stopped.

"Oh wow, here we are," Joanie said, rocking the car.

She put her weight behind the movement, laughing as they rocked violently above the white faces of the midway.

"Hey!" Mill said, the city's lights swirling before his eyes.

Her strong hands locked tightly on his leg, squeezing, and then slid upward, fingers dancing over his thigh.

"C'mon, let's do it up here," she said. "Maybe it'll be a first." Laughing, she slid her hand beneath his belt, fingertips almost reaching. Her hair fell loose across one side of her face, blown by the breeze from the river; her smile was slow and open and, Mill thought, terribly erotic. Fingers slid past his belt, closed on him and he leaned back, eyes shut. Far off a siren cried, and nearer the weird warnings of a tug boat, mysteries of the night. Beyond were houses filled with people, living out their separate miseries, their minor tragedies, all moving like a giant wheel through time toward death, that terminus. Tomorrow everything would be changed.

The machinery jerked, rocked, and too soon began to crank them down. Down into the warm air, the light, the smell of licorice and cotton candy. Down into the noise and laughter and shouts of children and barkers: *Yer don't play yer don't win!*

Later, they drove out of Oaks Park and across the river, the Ferris wheel a giant distorted ring blazing on the water. Mill leaned into the leather upholstery, pleased to be gliding through the night air in this noiseless machine. Across the bridge they turned left, heading south on the road that followed the road like a parallel stream. The trees grew together, branch to branch, over the road, like a bright tunnel in their headlights.

The road crested and Mill could see across the darkened valleys clear to Oregon City. His eye could follow the invisible trail of the Willamette upstream, through the lush greenery now couched in night. In another generation, he knew, this land would all be destroyed; all this natural beauty would be paved over by city planners and the architects of our time.

The road curved downward into Oswego. Joanie drove through the sleepy town, past the single traffic light, and around the lake. These were the houses Mill had once stared at in envy—huge mansions and rich cabanas, here at the edges of this calm, peaceful lake. Then he remembered that the lake was man-made, had been dug by hand by thousands of Chinese laborers at the turn of the century: the rich needed their workers.

Joanie stopped the car on a small promontory, the only space that seemed to not have a house on it. "C'mon," she said, grabbing the six-pack of beer, and easing her door shut. Mill followed her to the water's edge, and sat in the high grass. He took the beer she offered, tilted it, and tasted the salty beads of flavor against his tongue. The day had been a scorcher; he drank half the bottle at once, excited by the luxury of having his thirst slaked.

"What'll we do when they build a house here?"

"They won't," she said. "I own it."

"I should have guessed," Mill said. "Uncle Rathbone's land?"

He raised up on an elbow and slid his hand along her leg, feeling the enlarged calf muscle flex, the knee straighten its complex of small bones; over thigh, under the skirt. He heard her breath catch, loosen; felt her relax.

Then she was up, scrabbling to her feet to remove her blouse and skirt, kick off her shoes. Her bra and panties were luminous ghostly strips across her body, and then they were on the ground. "Come on," she said, walking into the still waters.

Mill emptied his beer, and shucked off his clothes. As he stepped into the water he could see Joanie swimming silently, almost to the float at which she aimed. He stepped into the darkness, the warm lake water rising against him. He pushed off, head up, swimming with wide breast strokes–he was a poor swimmer, but the float was only a couple hundred feet away. Eyes at water level, he saw the tops of Joanie's small ripples, and the lake surface, and, strangely distorted, the houses beyond, dark against the night.

Then, as his legs began to bunch up, he was at the float.

"Hey, I made it."

"Quiet," she said. "Sound carries. And I don't own this float."

He lay beside her, feeling the float rocking with their weight, and tried to get his breath. Without moving he touched her thigh, moist buttocks, arched spinal ridge. She rolled under his pressure and lay against him, her hands searching across his stomach, into the dark pubic hairs. Tired from the swim, his breath coming in clipped gasps, he could only lean into her, and feel her open under him. She shuddered, the float rolled, small waves churned toward shore. She stopped, and said, "Listen."

Mill heard a plane, high overhead, its lights invisible, its noise as remote as tomorrow's workday. Then he heard the sound of the lake, of water, and finally the creak of oarlocks, a boat, being rowed silently across dark water. Then he saw it, a rowboat, the single occupant a vague dark shadow, concerned with his task, whatever that might be.

They lay coupled in the night, unmoving, relaxed in their heat. Mill could sense every gentle ripple of Joanie's body, the slightest intention of her hips. He felt the beauty of a prolonged climax–they could lie here forever, or until morning, when all the citizens would rise for breakfast and look out at the strange sculpture.

Then the boat was gone, and Joanie pulled him to her, her hands grabbing his buttocks, holding him against her, legs tightening as she began to come, squeezing him as she came, and he felt himself released into her.

They lay quietly on the float until he diminished within her, and as she slid away she whispered: "Race you." She was in the water, her feet kicking silently against the planks, and as the float rocked back Mill pushed off. He chopped the water overhand for several fast strokes, and when he became winded he switched to a breast stroke, pushing handfuls of water away. Far ahead Joanie's luminescent wake raced toward shore, so Mill relaxed. He swam lazily in the warm water, saving his energy.

What about tomorrow? he wondered. He did not know what Joanie was thinking about. He didn't know yet how he had got tangled up with her in this way, what she saw in him, but they were comfortable together. Neither made any demand on the other.

Tomorrow–then he was thinking of how it would feel to wake up beside her every morning, to eat breakfast with her, to sit and watch TV in the evening. He could design and build a house for them, with a two-car garage and a game room. The fantasy grew, blossomed until he imagined himself working in the yard, painting rooms, fathering children–kids, never in his life had he thought about them.

But what if she *did* leave for Hydra, Acapulco, Mallorca?

He would call, only to hear the answering service.

Suddenly, he was out of air. He panicked, arms flailing, head going under. But the warm water was buoyant, and coming up he was on his back, arms easily rowing him toward the shore. The water covered his ears, and in this silence he was looking into the blackness at ten million stars.

Mill stepped from the shower, pleased that somehow it had become Friday evening, and that the day after tomorrow would be his day off. He and Joanie could drive to the beach or the Cascades for the whole day. Tonight Fronty had invited him over for a drink, along with the other old men, but if he were to leave early there might be a chance that he could phone Joanie. He wanted to see her.

As he reached for the towel he saw that same orchid car parked across the street. A tall, gangly boy moved toward the house, and was concealed behind the towering trees.

The doorbell was insistent, and because no one answered it Mill slipped into his underwear and slacks and skipped down the stairs. Through the front door he saw the blurred silhouette, topped with intense red hair, and when he opened it Mill faced a tanned, sinewy boy who looked like a born golfer.

"Hello, Audrey home? I'm J.J. Barnes."

"Well, I don't know," Mill said, looking over the boy's shoulder at the orchid car across the street. At first he had thought this was an assassin, and now calling for Audrey? "I just returned myself. I'll look out back." He was halfway across the living room before he thought to ask J.J. Barnes to come in. "Here's a book," he said, motioning to his father's scrap book of dreams.

Audrey and her mother were in the back yard, catching the last of the sun. They lay beside the rubble of the unfinished patio, his mother white, untanned, against the blue chaise lounge. Audrey rolled over at the sound of his voice and he saw, with surprise, that she had developed in this single summer. Her carriage had accelerated toward womanhood; it was a good bikini figure, and she tanned well, as her mother did not.

"Jay Jay," she said, clutching up her romance magazine and the amber bottle of lotion, kicking long legs out to bring her off the blanket. "Oh cripes, I forgot. Mom, I can't let him see me like this. Cripes."

"Audrey, go and get ready. I'll fix some ice tea, and Millard can talk to him."

"Oh cripes," Audrey said, pulling back a stray strand of hair, obviously pleased. "Mill, he'll want to talk about golf.

141

He's a sophomore at State, and works summers as a pro at the country club."

"I don't know anything about golf."

"Well, you know, talk about school."

But as they approached the house they heard their father's booming voice: "Pars and birdies all the way, but I held back on the last hole. Because you do not beat a man you want a contract from."

In the center of the front room Mr. Sederstrom was poised over a shiny iron; he wore Bermuda shorts, white net golf shirt, and a ventilated cap. When J.J. Barnes unkinked himself to give Mr. Sederstrom a pointer on how to grip the club, Mill noticed that they made a good twosome.

Audrey skirted the corner, waved, and pranced up the stairs; she did not have time to see what Mill saw.

"Dad," he said. "What for?"

Mr. Sederstrom sighted down the club, then raised his head. "Oh that," he said. He ran his finger along the uneven hairs on his upper lip, which would become a mustache. "Why not? Kinda makes me look like Clark Gable, don't you think?" His father waved the fat cigar, and then slipped it in place beneath the ragged mustache: he looked like a man who had got a good contract.

Mill went to his room and finished getting dressed. He sat in the sun that angled through the window, and as he pulled on clean socks he thought about the orchid colored car. It was clean, anyway–J.J. seemed the sort of person who kept everything in order. And where had he met Audrey? Mill had assumed that she didn't go out on dates.

Dressed, he shut the door to his room as Audrey's opened.

She stepped out, looking beautiful in a starched white blouse and printed skirt.

Mill gave a short whistle. "Your friend seems like a nice guy."

"Oh, he's real neat," she said, motioning with her hands.

They had hardly ever talked, and both felt uneasy here in the hallway. "I mean a good dresser, and careful, and smart, but not smart aleck. Why, after he got out of high school, Jay Jay spent two years working for the church. He's a Mormon," she said, as if that explained everything.

"Oh," Mill said, following her down the stairs. "Those guys who believe in polygamy."

"What?"

"Having a whole bunch of wives."

She turned to make a monkey face, which dissolved into a smile, and she was around the corner, exclaiming about her father's mustache.

In the kitchen his mother was finishing the supper dishes.

"I'm going over to Fronty's for a while," he said. "Probably be home early."

"Isn't Jay Jay a nice boy?" she asked. "Such a nice boy."

"Yes, he is," Mill said, and he closed the door on his mother's humming. He had *assumed* that Audrey never had dates, and now she was in the front room with Jay Jay, talking golf to her father. He had thought that he could help her, that she needed his help, and now she had someone else if help was needed.

The sun was a coal in the west, dying with full heat, as Mill cruised through the neighborhood. At Foster, he hit the gas, speed revving a warmish breeze past his head. Over the Galloping Goose tracks, past Inner's, where he noticed a man with a derby climb into a new Cadillac, and then down the straight, past Fronty's, which was locked tight, the CLOSED sign hanging askew in the window.

Up the mountain, into the dark night of the forest.

Fronty's house was a few rooms enclosed in knotty pine on two sides, tarpaper and lath on the other two. But it was a house one could relax in. It was surrounded by fir and cedar trees, and a creek cascaded down a stony bed into a small pool and waterfall beside the house; the rock garden was Margie's work. Behind the house, now concealed in high grass, were old cars and machinery—work Fronty had taken home long ago, and had never gotten around to doing.

Mill parked by the porch, in a row with Fronty's pickup and Gee-Eye's old military lorry. Snuff would be inside, and Inner would be here soon. All the old men.

"Come in," Fronty said. "Margie's gone. To bowl with some of her girl friends. To best utilize a free evening in which I said we'd tolerate no women. Come in."

Mill greeted Snuff and Gee-Eye, and accepted a glass of Snuff's homebrew. Gee-Eye rocked by the radio, foot tapping with the music. All but Mill heaved a heavy sigh, driven into senility by the heat and the drink.

"Where's Inner?" Fronty asked.

"He was at the yard when I passed," Mill said. "There was a new Cad out front—do you suppose he's floated a loan to clear out his yard and stock it with wrecked sports cars? Exclusively."

Snuff giggled at this idea, and Fronty shook his head, and Gee-Eye began to announce his plan for getting rich, which was to buy a government surplus landing craft and a couple barges and take all Inner's steel directly to Japan, to sell it, when Inner's truck steamed up the hill. Soon the wrecker pitched through the door, a jug of Greeneye in each hand.

"I'm out."

As Inner sagged to the first chair, Snuff turned off the radio and Fronty shoved a piston cup between the two jugs and Mill asked: "Out?" Inner poured himself a cup, tossed the Greeneye down, and refilled it.

When the little knives hit his stomach, he said: "Out. Through. Done." He surveyed the four faces, and finished the terrible confession, "I done sold out."

"Sold the yard?" Fronty asked.

"I'll be damned," Mill said.

"Good for you," Gee-Eye said, because he had been in business for seventeen years, and had been sixteen trying to get out.

"How'd it happen?" Fronty asked.

144

"It just happened," Inner said; he heaved a great sigh as he realized that he had no responsibilities—that he was a free man, unfettered. "At four this gentleman came by, and without even looking the place over he shoved a legal paper under my nose. He wished to buy the property, and the cornfield, which I own. He intends to build a huge shopping center. No dickering. By the time I had my glasses on to read the fine print, I knew I'd sell. I knew I'd sell out." Another cup of Greeneye went down, untasted.

Mill said, "I'll be damned."

"It's over now," Fronty said, his brow knitted into lines.

"What could I do?" Inner protested. "I figgered, for thirty-four years I've worked the land, now I'll let the land work for me."

"You will, of course, still be interested in the Sports Special?" Mill asked.

"Nossir. Not at all," Inner said. Now fortified by the Greeneye and a sense of triumph, he drew himself up straight, a respectable man. Tomorrow and the next day, he would regret signing the bill of sale, but he would regret it less and less until the rows of wrecks faded from his thoughts. "It's time to re-tire, like the tire ad says. Nope, I'm going to California. I'm getting out of this town and going to where the big money is. And the sunshine. I'm getting out of this rain—going to where there's less weather and more climate."

"That's it," Fronty said. "It's over."

"I had to do it," Inner said. "For the money, and the chance to get out. Oh, I could have made plenty of money during the war. I could have sold the gas stamps that went with every car I got. Could have sold the tires on the black market. Could have sold gas stamps and ration books and tires, but I didn't. Not patriotic Inner. Nossir. So I missed one big chance then; I don't dare miss another. Better think what you'll do if this feller wants your place. You'll sell."

Fronty was silent, and Mill thought, No he won't, and then as he saw the old racer's cheeks puff and withdraw, he thought, Maybe. Then he knew: Fronty would sell.

For Fronty would not allow himself to become manager of a new company built station, with its sterile glass and stone facade and sanitary oil displays and silent lube rack; Fronty could never accept a station that depended upon trading stamps and credit cards and billboards. No, Fronty would sell, and he would not even be offered a managership, because he was a hopeless cripple. He would open a small garage in his backyard; he would make no profit, of course, and finally he would fade into Social Security.

"Man O Man," Gee-Eye said. "I'd sell in a minute."

"Sure you would," Inner agreed. "I done it."

Mill finished the homebrew, then drank the cup of Greeneye that was raised to toast Inner's success; when the liquor hit his stomach, Mill felt the terrible finality. Monday a portable press would rear its crusher head over the rows of rusting wrecks, to gobble them body, chassis, and engine total, and would eject perfect squares of baled junk, ready for the smelter. A bulldozer would scoop miscellaneous debris into a pile, and a huge fire would consume whatever would burn. That leaning board fence would go in last, and an era would end.

But before this passed, and long before the bulldozers and earth movers appeared, before the ground was cleared and leveled, foundations poured and steel erected, Inner would be in California, swimming in sun and drink and prosperity—*and here's to a prosperous piece.* He would be a sloppy, happy old junker in a hundred dollar suit, and with his money he would find friends.

Yesterday all Inner had was a hubcap full of coins, money he had found penny by penny under the backseats of wrecked cars—and tomorrow he would have thousands.

When Mill pushed back his chair to go, it was Inner's action that stirred him. He took several steps, and when the old men continued their chatter Mill went out the door into the night–past Inner's beat up tow truck, Fronty's pickup, and Gee-Eye's old military lorry, and he headed the roadster down the hill.

In this forest it was night; trees melted in his headlights. The breeze of motion carried the scent of spruce and fir over the chopped windshield. Mill hit the gas, sent the stubby roadster leaping ahead: he wanted to get into the city, to be among lights and people. He wanted to phone Joanie, and unless her answering service was on the other end he would ask her to meet him–somewhere.

The old men would endure; he could not remain part of their Past. Epoch followed epoch, and although there would be some overlapping or intrusions, any upheaval brought a geological dividing line: for Mill the absolute demarcation was the loss of Inner's yard. An historical landmark gone, in the name of progress.

Headlights ducked a curve and approached quickly from behind.

First he thought, Police. When the car loomed in his mirror he realized the lights fell at an angle from the scoop nosed, raked body, and he heard the dual exhausts accelerating. Realizing this, he shoved the gear lever into second, but the Mercury sedan was nudging his nerf bar.

Then the roadster began a frantic, painless scream as the engine revved into a tight, ever winding knot; the Merc was left behind, but over the engine's scream Mill could hear the curses.

Marty's Merc: inside were Eddie, Gus, the whole bunch, including Tonto, no doubt. *Yore goin to get the meat.*

Mill kept the gas to the floor, wound the engine tight in second and shifted to high, still accelerating; he feared that raked, gutted Mercury and the juvenile mob it contained.

He passed a cresting curve quickly and was at the junction of three roads before the Merc's lights appeared. He swung the roadster wide and took the sharp right turn in a broadslide that carried him to the ditch's lip; power brought him back, rear wheels screaming under traction. He cut his lights and coasted around the corner, engine idling, listening. They would not go straight because they wouldn't be able to see his taillights; they might turn left, or right.

Over the sound of his idling engine, Mill heard tree frogs, erratic in their saw-tooth harmony. When he sensed the whisper of tires on asphalt, Mill dropped the gear lever into first—but before his skimming, squealing tires shattered the stillness, like a covey of quail wheeling up the hill, he knew that the Merc had cut its lights and had coasted around the corner, in his very tracks.

The Merc's gutted mufflers reverberated against the forest, one second before Mill's engine revved alive; dual beams of light pinpointed him on the road. He shoved the gas to the floor and was gone, but as his spinning tires gained traction a spider web appeared etched neatly on his windshield. Instantly, reflected in his mirror, there followed a tongue of flame, and the gun's report.

The roadster streaked into the first curve and Mill flipped the headlight toggle switch. Fragments of safety-glass dropped into the cockpit, enlarging a hole just .32 caliber.

The road stretched straight, and as he reached the next curve a flame winked in his mirror; the bullet whirred close overhead, to spend itself somewhere in the forest.

Fear knotted his stomach as the turns raced at him, faster and tighter and darker. Instinct urged him down the speedball black highway; he drove hard and fast, and more skillfully than he ever thought possible. He did not want to wreck the roadster because he loved it, and because then they would get him dead or alive.

In the next straight the Merc's lights struck the back of his head; a bullet slammed into the roadster, an impetus that sent it hurtling around the curve as if the car rode on rails.

Then he was hopelessly lost, and roared toward an unknown safety. No house lights winked from the trees; no cars passed him. His gas gauge read half full, and with the thin margin of road between the two cars he hoped to head back toward town: lights, cars, people, the police.

As the fourth bullet zoomed through the air, Mill was reviewing his life, his mistakes and what seemed possible–in that split-second he was thinking of Joanie, and although it would never have happened anyway he was thinking of a house somewhere, a TV set, dinners on the patio; he was thinking of things possible and impossible as the fourth bullet hit the right rear tire. The car was on the lip of the curve and it angled sharply, like a wedge driven into the road. When Mill put the gas pedal to the floor the back end sloshed without response, sliding toward the ditch; he fought to right the car's drift, squared it with the road, and when he had control he floorboarded the gas. The deflated tire wobbled, and under acceleration the tire peeled from the rim, to roll beside the spinning car and past it, into the brush.

The roadster cartwheeled slowly into a centrifugal slide, sideways, then backwards, then nose first into the ditch, bouncing with a gentleness that Mill hadn't expected. When the car had nearly stopped, half on, half off the road, the right front corner dropped into nothing and the roadster pitched upward and sideways, throwing Mill across the seat and over the passenger's door.

Mill tasted the damp grass and struggled to his feet, shaking his head to clear it. The engine had died but Mill reached into the car to turn off the ignition, and as he stood beside the car what he noticed most was the absolute silence. After the screaming chase and the tire-ripping curves, the silence was almost oppressive; he heard only the faintest breeze rustling the tree tops, like a low moan.

Ten feet away the Merc waited, engine cut. Mill stood in the twin hoops of light, waiting for the bullet that would smash through the crosshairs of his sternum, where the two beams met.

What were Fronty's words? That's it. It's all over now.

"Like, you lost the race, man."

Marty stepped into the light, his cycle cap cocked low over waves of hair, his tight jacket sleeve tapering down to the hand with the gun. "Tonto drove real good, don'tcha think?"

Tonto drove– Mill slumped against the roadster's cowl, feeling the car shift under his elbow; he heard voices from the darkness, car doors opening, the Merc's radio blasting into the country air. Mill recognized the figure that slouched forward. Eddie hung onto Tonto's arm; her other hand held onto Gus, who walked in motorcycle leathers, looking like a young Gestapo officer.

"Listen, Tonto," Mill said. "Call off these punks. You don't belong with them–"

"O help us, Mister," a faceless voice whined, mocking him. "Straighten us punks out."

Mill stopped: he wanted to tell Tonto how wrong he had been, but there was no response from the darkness around the Mercury. Tonto stood in the pale of light, expressionless, silent. Mill saw two figures move away from the group and disappear beside the road.

"Okay," he said, straightening his aching body. "I'll play your game."

"What game?" Marty said. "We just want to talk. You wouldn't stop to talk so we stopped you. Before you got caught speeding. Wouldn't want the big teacher to get a ticket. Give you a bad rep."

"Yeah, the big teacher," a voice said nearby. A short, stocky kid stepped forward to give Mill a fast, hard blow on the shoulder. Mill stared as the boy danced back, a fat kid Mill had never seen before.

"The big man," said Gus, moving sideways to get behind Mill. "The big-assed man."

Eddie ran into the darkness and Mill heard the door open; she turned the Merc's radio on full blast, a full-race accolade of hard-rock: music to kill by. Sound filled the forest, shifted in hard waves over the closing circle of kids, and Mill pressed tightly against the car. He fought down fear, and the desire to run.

"Let's dance, man," a kid said. "Rockit."

"You dance, big-ass?" Marty asked. "Let's see if you shake it pretty good." He aimed the pistol at the ground and fired, the flat bark of the bullet buzzing off the pavement. A hole appeared beside Mill's foot, and he jumped back.

Eddie was dancing in the glare of the Merc's lights, twisting to the full-race bebop radio, rotating in the unreal glare as the bullet ricocheted into the night.

Eddie pushed Tonto forward, sent him sprawling into Marty. "Go ahead," she said, "give your brother what you promised."

When Tonto tripped against Marty, throwing him off balance, Mill saw his chance: he lunged, arm cocked, and swung overhand, his wild fist smashing Marty's jaw. They fell together to the road, wrestling for the gun; Mill saw the fat kid reel away as if he had been hit. The sudden attack gave Mill time to hit Marty three, four blows; grabbing handfuls of the long greasy hair he repeatedly knocked Marty's head against the road.

As the gun passed to Mill's hand, he felt the side of his head explode in pain, blood, anger, fear; Gus stepped back to kick again with his iron-shod cycle boot.

"He gave *me* the meat," Eddie screamed, dancing in the Merc's headlights, her hard tight body rocking to the radio's charivari.

She danced past in the ghostly light, beyond Marty's still form, the animal eyes of the gang that glowed from the forest. Mill slowly turned to see Gus's boot swinging like a pendulum, the steel plate bright as chrome, the leg foreshortened, the leathers black and evil. Slowly the boot swung, caught Mill on the shoulder, rolling him over.

The starry night exploded. The gun had slipped away, clattering off into the brush. Mill jumped to his feet, head bursting with colors and pain, the street like a trampoline beneath him. Growing larger, Gus arched his arm into a bow; the blow passed overhead, and Mill swung hard into the thick motorcycle leathers, felt the radius of pain as he connected with the massive belt buckle.

"Hot licks," Eddie screamed, dancing from light to shadow, a rocker rally girl. "Everybody gets hot licks."

Light diffused over the backs of the gang; they stepped over Marty, who moaned gently, and stopped, a row of clenched fists, mean faces. Then Mill saw the motorcycle boot coming up, felt its tip catch him in the crotch. He reeled back, the hand of broken fingers holding his nuts; the fire raced and diminished, in cycles, from madness to sanity, like seasons turning quickly in his mind.

Then he saw the gun.

It lay a foot from Marty's head, steel blue in the car lights. As Gus moved in, hovering, his arms bound by the leathers which allowed only short chopping blows, Mill ducked behind the roadster; the gang all ran to the back of the car to head him off, but Mill dropped low, slipped, fell, got up and turned, racing around the car's grill to throw himself full length into the street, sliding to the weapon.

His hand fit the grips, his finger fumbled, found the trigger, cold and curved. For a moment, as he began to roll over to cover the gang, he thought everything was all right, he knew he could shoot, if necessary—as he began the slow roll, drugged with pain, he was hit from above, his face driven into the blacktop. The gun clattered away; his head burst, he tasted blood, gravel, his own tongue.

He looked up to see Tonto's disembodied face, grim, sneering, contemptuous, his foot raised to kick again.

Mill was spread-eagled on the road and they were all on him: a pile of silent, efficient killers, slugging, drop-kicking, driving knees and elbows and fists into him.

Mill felt a hundred pain points, and it seemed to take forever to pass out. The last image he saw, before night closed in, was Eddie clawing at his face, screaming: "Give the sonvabitch the meat!"

The sun spreads across the open, celebrated fields. Dew webs weave sharp patterns in the grass, and like stars of memory goldenrod and dandelion burst into a new morning.

The open field spreads to cascades to infinity, from his own front porch to the corrugated basalt of Mt. Hood, blue and white in the distance. The road is a tan trail, and its pockets hold the fine dust of summer—light alluvium, which lifts on the cool morning breeze, but which will not stain any Monday wash. The air is almost summer, cloudless and blue, and even at noon the sun's warmth will be comfortable. The grass sways gently, warm air rises, and the day generates a lazy energy.

Beside the telephone pole a boy mounts a bicycle. He is wearing only bathing trunks and no shoes, and his actions are cautious: he leans the bike against the pole and climbs hand over hand across the sprocket and frame to the seat, where he rests, still gripping the pole. One pedal is straight up, and as he pushes the telephone pole away his foot comes down hard on this pedal—these are the overtures to motion, and teetering the fat balloon tires accept the rider's balance. The wheels duck into pockets and out again, as progress is traced by the thin plume of dust. The bike is far too big for the boy, yet he rides. And will ride and ride all morning within the limits of this dusty road, because he can't get off. Tomorrow perhaps he will learn to dismount without falling.

Where that tan trail blazes like a mirage another boy, older, comes into view; he leans against the rope slung over one shoulder, pulling a rusty, gutted Model-A roadster whose wheels buck and fall from rut to rut. Dust does not cushion the rattles of flapping fenders, nor soften the glow of crimson rust. The boy strains against the rope, against the balky car, against the lazy day. The street has no houses, and so no one sees the car rise and fall at the end of a rope, following ruts to the boy's backyard where it will be carefully disassembled.

Mill woke as the Merc's tail lights faded into the night. In his head the dual exhausts still roared. His body ached, and would ache more when he moved. His mouth was filled with the strong taste of blood and gravel. At least he had not been cut, the meat that Eddie wanted.

When the Mercury was gone, Mill forced himself up on his elbows, to crawl across the pavement an inch at a time. With a curious desire for self-examination, he probed with his tongue the jagged gap where two teeth had been.

He got to the side of the road, where he would not be run over, and saw the roadster, tilted to its shadow. The moonlight picked up millions of tiny depressions, and flung them back like stars: a galaxy of tiny pits covered every inch of the body, and in places the lacquer paint was lifted away.

The body was totaled.

Then he passed out again, in the shadow of the car, but not before he remembered having heard the sound of rain: they had used their gang weapons for revenge, their lug-studded belts and cycle chains. They had smashed the car with these, and the noise had come to his ears like wedges of water falling on metal.

When he woke again strong arms were under him; the light in his eyes was red, a film of hemorrhage. A light that pumped red in spurts like an artery, over the road, the people, the brush.

He was shoved into the front seat of the police car; the second officer came down the road from where he had placed the red flare, a candle of phosphorous that would burn until the tow truck came.

Mill stared dully at the farmer who surveyed the action: coming home late, he had found this boy after the accident. Racing, no doubt, on this empty road. Yes, lucky he'd passed. Else the boy might've laid here three, four days. But a strange accident, and the policeman noticed it too: the car freshly pitted and buckled, yet nearly upright; and the boy so badly banged up on all sides, as if he'd been in a series of accidents.

"Listen," Mill mumbled, his jaws not working. "Tow the car to Fronty's Garage. Got that? Fronty's."

The farmer nodded, and mentally paced off the long black skid mark. "I'll do that."

"Crazy bastard," the driver said, carefully turning the car around and streaking down the hillside. He flipped a switch on the dash, and the overhead light ceased to pump blood. "Racing. Every night we see them. Crazy hopped up kids and cars."

Chapter 11

At Mill's back the police car accelerated away, and he teetered, walked drunkenly toward the curb. The laughter of bean pickers fell into silence as he swayed, his foot raised high, preparing for that giant step that would lift him across two lanes of traffic. The pavement was unsteady, and after the heated police car he felt the cold breeze that cut through his torn shirt.

Curb and sidewalk came closer, but a single step seemed to take hours. The gray rim of concrete, which separated street from what wasn't, seemed to recede and spring forward. This, he felt, was an illusion caused by the poor light of the false dawn.

On the curb the bean pickers waited in dusty clothes for the bus that would carry them to fields along the Columbia. They were a motley group, high school students and pensioners, wearing bandanas and wide straw hats; at each pair of feet, like obedient puppies, sat lunch buckets. The faces that watched were the color of ashes. They saw his feet rise in exaggerated motions of walking, as if he were afraid he might trip over a car roof.

Through the window of the police car he had heard them laughing, and he knew why they laughed: today the weather would be fine for field work. The morning was chilly and the day would be cool. The first sign of the winter to come. Beyond the solstice, the sun would begin to diminish, to cant its heat toward the southern hemisphere; the blue skies would haze into the light gray of Indian Summer and after the first killing frost would come months of cold rain.

There were no cars on Foster Road at this early hour and he knew that he would get across, given enough time. Still, if he had not stepped out of that police car he would now be home in bed, sleeping off the sedatives. If he were asleep he would not know this dizzy rush of air at his ears, nor the pain that followed bone marrow like a current though a wiring diagram.

The pickers had seen him leave the police car, and now their ashen faces were set in grim lines; when he got over the curb the murmur was not a muffled cheer but whispered complaints. Mill shuffled past them, back erect, head high, as if he were out for a stroll and not stumbling recklessly. His eyes were on Hubert's (Open All Nite) Drive-Inn, where, from the police car, he had seen the battered '49 Ford. In this cool dawn there was no full-race radio, no humping belly-skidding dancers. Before the light had flicked to green Mill had said: "I've got a friend here. I'll make it home."

And now he was not so sure that he would.

But what he remembered from last night, between the vision of the boy playing in open fields and the nightmare sequence of death, was the sound of their torture instruments falling like rain on the roadster, and, before his brain skidded into a metallic darkness, Tonto's voice, crying: *No, not the car. Not the car.*

The sun rose behind him, and as he shoved open Hubert's door he saw the mirrored image of his destruction. He ignored the sleepy, sleazy carhop and the tired cook, and walked to the center of the room.

There were six in the curved booth. Tonto, Marty, Gus, and three others; no laughter rocked the room, the jukebox was silent. The boy facing the door nudged Tonto, and the half-circle of faces revolved to see a stiff-legged, raked figure, one fist clenched, his face raging beneath bandages. Mill took two steps forward, to teeter at the booth's edge. One at a time they'd have to come out, and as they emerged half-bent he could drive a shoe into a crotch, his good fist into a face.

"Why'd you wreck it?" he asked.

The three closest turned their backs, and the others looked at their Cokes or the cups of their own hands.

157

"No trouble," the cook said, coming around the counter, tattoos bulging over his upper arms. "Take yer fight outside."

"No fight," Mill said, waving him away. "No fight. Give me a coffee, black."

"You sonofabitch," Tonto screamed, suddenly trying to climb out of the booth. "If you'd driven good they'd never got the car." As the boy on each side pulled Tonto down, his screams became long sobs, and he was crying furiously. "The goddamn car was the best thing you ever done."

Tonto's skinny frame hunched over the table and when his head dropped on his arms the two shoulder blades protruded like breasts, or angel wing nubs. Mill jerked his thumb at the others, and one by one the gang slid from the booth; they stared at their own shoes and although Marty and Gus swaggered weakly no one spoke.

Mill took his coffee and sat across from his brother, hearing the intense sobs, the sharp intake of breath; he knew the pain Tonto felt. For seven years, while Mill was in the army and away at school, the boy had seen the roadster in the garage, the only evidence that his older brother existed. And as he looked at the car he dreamed: no doubt he saw himself in it at drive-ins, waiting at stoplights, sitting in the school parking lot. Mill knew how such dreams became obsessions.

"Okay," Mill said, relenting. "Take it easy."

"Fuck you, big ass." Tonto turned a tear-stained cheek toward Mill. "All I heard from the Old Man was how great it'd be when you got home. No more worries. Driving a big car. Wow, what a load of shit. All I got when you came back was to sleep on the couch."

"Pop said that?" Mill sucked at his coffee with aching lips. He hadn't known that his father had promised so much; now he could recognize more clearly the family's disappointment. Especially Tonto's disappointment: for seven years the car had served as a dream and reminder of the brother and what magic he could do. When Mill had

158

returned, a failure by their standards, the dream diminished and faded.

Mill reached into his pocket and laid a quarter beside the cup; he reached in again and laid the car's ignition key on the table. "Here," he said, sliding the key across. "You rebuild that car. It won't be easy, but it can be done. You go to work for Fronty—today, this morning—and he'll help you work on the roadster."

Painfully Mill got to his feet and started for the door.

He turned and said: "It better be good work, too." Then he was outside, in the clean air. His head was beginning to throb as if a small motor up there was being started. He moved toward the corner, now empty of bean pickers, shuffling slowly.

Tomorrow, he would—do nothing. Sleep for a week, read a bit, stare out the window where the trees would be changing to the next season. Perhaps then he would begin to look for a job, or perhaps he would return to school, since on a day like this the air had the tinge of fall that he had always liked when walking across campus.

What he would do for certain he didn't know; he only knew that right now he was going home, to sleep.

He took the bus.

About the Author

Albert Drake was born in Portland, Oregon when it was less populous and life had the quality of Norman Rockwell paintings. He was educated in public schools and followed his father's footsteps, working for years in service stations, garages and automotive warehouses. He eventually attended Portland State College, and got his degrees at the University of Oregon. He twice won the Ernest Haycox Prize for fiction. For nearly 30 years he labored in the groves of academe, where he was cited for his outstanding teaching and rose to the rank of Full Professor. He was the first academic to teach a class in science fiction as literature, and for several years he was Director of the Clarion Science Fiction Workshop. He has received numerous academic and creative grants, including two major grants from the National Endowment for the Arts. His fiction, poetry and prose have been widely published in literary quarterlies and popular magazines, including *Redbook*, *Epoch*, *North American Review* and *The Best American Short Stories*. He is currently Professor Emeritus of English.

.

Books by Albert Drake

Poetry
Michigan Signatures (Ed) (1969)
Riding Bike (1973)
Cheap Thrills (1975)
Rustfire (1975)
Returning to Oregon (1975)
Garage (1981)
Homesick (1988)

Fiction
The Postcard Mysteries (1975)
Tillamook Burn (1977)
In the Time of Surveys (1978)
I Remember the Day James Dean Died (1983)

Novels
One Summer (1979)
Beyond the Pavement (1981)

Non-Fiction
Street Was Fun in '51 (1982)
The Big "Little GTO" Book (1982)
A 1950's Rod & Custom Builder's Wishbook (1985)
Herding Goats (1989)
Hot Rodder!: From Lakes to Street (1993)
Flat Out (1994)
Fifties Flashback (1998)
Portland Pictorial: The 1950s (2006)
Northwest Oldtimers (2007)
Age of Hot Rods (2008)
Jacket & Plaque (2008)
Christmas at Ed's Richfield (2009)
Overtures to Motion (2011)

www.flatoutpress.com

www.ingramcontent.com/pod-product-compliance
Lightning Source LLC
Chambersburg PA
CBHW071937170626
46813CB00005B/1771